The Future According to Danny Higgins

SEAMUS MCQUAID

authorHOUSE®

AuthorHouse™ UK
1663 Liberty Drive
Bloomington, IN 47403 USA
www.authorhouse.co.uk
Phone: UK TFN: 0800 0148641 (Toll Free inside the UK)
       UK Local: 02036 956322 (+44 20 3695 6322 from outside the UK)

Published by AuthorHouse 08/17/2021

ISBN: 978-1-6655-9124-9 (sc)
ISBN: 978-1-6655-9133-1 (e)

Library of Congress Control Number: 2021916934

CHAPTER 1

A BEAUTIFUL INNOCENCE

Danny and Bosco peered through a hole in the hedge "Any minute now" announced Danny. "Any minute"

"She mightn't be about today", suggested Bosco.

"Oh! She's there alright I know by the way he's acting", Danny replied.

Jip the collie dog was slowly making his way down the field. He was walking as if in slow motion, lifting one foot slowly, leaving it down before lifting the next, appearing behind every rush bush as he went.

"Ach, I doubt if she's there", Bosco said, normally it would be all over by now".

The words hadn't left his lips when Jip made a spring forward and in the same instance a large brown hare rose and sprinted across the field followed by Jip yelping in pursuit. Danny and Bosco ran down to a wooden gate to have a better view of the proceedings.

"What did I tell you", said Danny. "She gets mighty craic tormenting that poor dog of ours. Go on boy your closing in on her".

Bosco laughed. "You say that every morning but the sad fact is she pulls away all the time. If he'd stop barking and put his whole energy into running he might have a chance of catching her".

"You and I know well he'll not catch her but we should still encourage him", suggested Danny.

The hare made its way to a hole in the hedge and skipped on to the road. She wasn't in any great panic. She casually made her way fifty yards along the road and turned up McNamee's lane. Meanwhile the dog was having difficulty finding a hole to let him through. Eventually he followed the hare up the lane now some distance behind.

"Cripes! They're away up our lane", cried Bosco, if the auld fella is about the yard he'll go crazy".

Just then a terrible racket occurred on McNamee's yard. Squaking hens were flying everywhere as the hare and Jip crossed over, then a man's raised voice shouting obscenities could be plainly heard by the two lads.

"What did I tell you", said Bosco. "Some morning he'll be waiting for them with the gun and blow them to smithereens".

The two animals then disappeared and a short time later Jip with his tongue hanging returned to the crossroads.

"Game over for another day Jip", said Danny. "I think I'll give that dog to a greyhound breeder to train".

"My advice", said Bosco, is to give him to a greyhound breeder alright to feed his dogs for a day or so. He must be a big age now".

"About ten years old", answered Danny, "too old to be running after hares".

Danny kicked a stone down the road. "What were we talking about before that racket started"? Oh! aye, I was saying Alice and I are going to the pictures tonight and her cousin Susan is coming as well".

"Are you paying both of them in", queried Bosco.

"Ah! no bloody way I'm meeting them inside Do you think I'm made of money. I find it difficult enough to raise my own two bob".

Bosco smiled. "Your always telling me the nice girl Alice is and the great notion you have of her. It mustn't be that fantastic when you wouldn't spend two shilling on her".

"Well she'd expect me to pay Susan in aswell", said Danny. "They could be looking for chips after and I don't have that kind of money".

"The last of the big spenders", taunted Bosco.

"Ive been thinking you could do worse than join us", replied Danny. "I'm meeting them in the back row of the two shilling seats on the right side. We could cycle into the town together. I'll enter first and then when the picture starts and the place is in darkness you can arrive. They'll think it's just coincidence that were sitting near each other. When the lights comes up after the ads I'll call over to you. You can come over and I'll introduce you to them. You could do worse. Susan is a nice wee girl and if she's like her cousin she'll be full of passion".

Bosco let a giggle. "So that's why your seeing so much of Alice".

"One of the reasons", answered Danny. "Come on man and take a chance, you wouldn't know what would develop out of it".

"Ach! I don't know I wouldn't know Susan. Is she the youngest of the Friels? Small, a bit plump, red hair"

"That's her", said Danny. "The way you describe her, you'd think she was a turkey for Christmas. (making fun) "Do you know Mrs she'll be very tasty cause she's small and plump". They both burst out laughing.

"I know the oldest sister. She's a fine looking lassie", commented Bosco. "She sings in the choir on Sundays".

"Aye, she's a smasher but she's away in Dublin studying to be a doctor or a vet or maybe both" answered Danny.

"That could be handy", Bosco replied. She could come out and see your granny's pains and then your da could have her examine a sick cow, handy alright".

Why don't you come and see how things pan out", coaxed Danny. "The picture "A kid for two farthings" looks interesting as well.

"I'll see", said Bosco, but I can't promise you anything".

A car come along the road driving slowly and turned by Higgins lane.

Danny stared after the car "Who the devil is visiting our house so early in the morning, a green A40".

"It's a bit like Father McManus's car, said Bosco. "But why would he be visiting your house at this time of the day. Maybe he's there to tell your parents about you and Alice (mimicking Father McManus) "Mr and Mrs Higgins I bring you terrible news about your son, Daniel. He is company keeping with John McAree's daughter from the other side of the town. It has been brought to my attention that they frequently frequent the back row of the two shilling seats in the local cinema". Danny butts in. " It's my understanding that a considerable amount of moaning and groaning can be clearly heard coming from this area, and I've been informed by Miss Flynn an observant spinister who resides near McAree's how she has witnessed him leaving Miss McAree home on the bar of his bike quite late at night. He then kisses her several times before mounting.......... his cycle and disappearing". They both burst out laughing.

"I'm away home in case it's him, I'll have to state my case", said Danny. "Try and make tonight, we'll have a bit of craic".

Bosco turns to go "I'll try my best but as you well know if the auld fella wants something done I'll not be going anywhere".

Every morning after the cows were milked, it was their job to bring the creamery can of milk to Con's crossroads and set it on the milk stand ready to be lifted by Tommy Anderson's lorry, then delivered to the creamery. They would then stand for a while and discuss current news and latest goings on. Sometimes the discussions could be long and varied but the theme would usually be confined to football, dances, films or girls.

As Danny approached the lane the green car made its way onto the road and travelled towards the town. "Strange one", he thought. "But all will be revealed". His thoughts turned to the two girls again. If only he could coax Bosco to hook up with Susan it would solve a few problems.

Danny wasn't happy at not paying Alice into the cinema but he wouldn't have the money to pay her and Susan in, as well as purchasing chips for them afterwards. He wished he could afford it but the bottom line was he couldn't. "My mother, god love her", he thought, "Does her best by giving me a few bob a week but it's not hard to spend. The simple fact is, there is no surplus of money about the house".

CHAPTER 2

Tess took another look down the lane. "No word of him yet"? queried Danny's Granny. "No" answered Tess.

Granny wiggled in her chair. "Dan you'll have to have a word with him or leave the milk can down at the crossroads yourself. That's every morning those two stand spoofing. Or what do they be talking about. Every week it seems to get longer. He has no consideration for anyone making a breakfast".

"I see Johney the Spade coming down the back lane. Are you getting him to do something"? enquired Tess.

"The meadow at Flanagan's March could do with a few drains", explained Dan.

"Would it not be more sensible to have Danny digging them instead of paying a man?", questioned Granny "Between football, dancing and them damned pictures, he'll soon have no time to do any work".

"Ach well, said Dan, "Johney doesn't cost the earth".

Johney the Spade's right name was Johney Brennan, a simple gentle sort of man. He earned his living by doing bits and pieces mostly digging with a spade. He had his own spade and cared for it like a child. No one was really sure where he came from but for the last twenty years or so he lived in a hovel with very little comforts. He didn't look for much payment and indeed was taken advantage of quite a bit.

"Ah! Johney just in time for a drop of tea", said Tess, "you'll eat a egg?

Johney placed his spade wrapped in a jute bag carefully inside the door. "Mrs Higgins I'd love an egg if you have one to spare, if you don't mind". "The weather has picked up a bit from last week Dan".

"Indeed it has, your still kept busy"? Dan asked.

"Aye indeed I done work for the Gorman brothers, just completed it yesterday".

Tess gave the egg she had for Danny to Johney and put on another one. Johney tucked into the food and it was easy to see it was his first bite that day. Tess came in from having another look to see if Danny was coming.

"I see a green car coming up the lane", said Tess. "I wonder who could it be at this time of the day".

"It might be a byre inspector, they have said they're going to increase their visits", said Dan.

A man descended from the car and came to the open door. The man explained he was from the Electricity Board and he was looking for a Danny Higgins.

"What has he done now"? Granny asked sharply.

The man laughed. "I have a feeling you think he's in trouble, but no, he sent us a list of names from around these parts who'd be interested in having electricity installed. We have it a couple of months but are only getting around to dealing with it now". He takes a letter from the folder he was carrying and reads, Dear Sir or Madam, Below are the names of our neighbours who have shown interest in having electricity installed. The fella then read out the dozen or so names which was on the list. Most lived in the surrounding areas. For a few seconds after he finished a silence fell over the house.

Eventually Dan spoke "Have you talked to any of these people"? "Not yet", the man said. "I thought I'd better interview the person at the source of the letter first".

"Well I can promise you Sir, the person at the source of the letter won't be getting any electricity installed", assured Dan. "He's a son of mine and unless he can pay for it himself which I think is highly unlikely, it won't be happening".

Granny butted in "Go and interview all the people on that list and everyone will tell you the same thing. They don't want anything to do with electricity for the good reason, they couldn't afford it".

The man tried to explain that it mightn't be as expensive as they'd think. Dan asked him if he could give him some ideas on cost "Well it would all depend on how many signs up. If everyone goes for it I'd estimate about three hundred pounds".

Granny piped up again. "And where do you think we'd get three hundred pounds on eighteen acres of bad land. As well as that there's a few scoundrals on that list, they'd take it alright but would they pay, I don't think so. Ray Mohan, Jack Delaney, Andy of the Hollow. They wouldn't buy food for themselves".

"Now", said Tess, "you shouldn't say such things"

"It's the truth I'm saying Andy of the hollow starved his own mother to death before he'd buy food for her" "Well", said the man, "they have to sign a contract and if they didn't pay ………"

"There" answered Granny. "Do you hear that, you have to sign a contract and they'd have you where they wanted you.

Again the man tried to make a case for having electricity but to no avail. Dan butted in "If we were going down that road we'd have to borrow out of the bank and that's not going to happen, we've been farming here over seventy years and we never borrowed money and we'll not be starting now.

The man realised it was a lost cause. "Why don't you talk it over for a few weeks and maybe you'll find it mightn't be such a bad idea. In the meantime I'll interview some of these other clients on the list. Here's my card give me a ring if you reconsider".

Dan wiped his mouth. "I don't think you'll be hearing from us.

Tess left him to the door "I'm sorry this lad has lead you on a wild goose chase".

The man let a giggle. "It's all in a day's work for me Mrs Higgins. Ive seen this situation before and then in a few year's time I'd be back signing them all up".

As he slowly made his way out of the lane on to the road, he spied a young lad and a dog coming down the road. "He is most likely to be the source of the letter", he thought. He was in two minds whether to stop or not but decided to move on. "It wouldn't help the situation, that fella isn't going to have his way at least not for a while yet", he thought, "but some day he will"

As Danny sauntered down the road he saw the green car turn towards the town. "Must be some bloke selling something", he thought. His mind then turned to the time of year, March. The days were getting longer and warmer. The football was beginning on Sunday. He hoped he could hold down a place on the team this year. After all he was now eighteen and had done well enough last year.

His Father and Johney were just finishing their breakfast.

"How's she cutting Johney boy? Danny enquired "There's rumours going around the country that you've purchased a new pocket watch". "I have indeed. I sent away for it out of Cassie Byrne's catalogue. I'm giving her a shilling a month", boasted Johney. He takes the watch out of his pocket, "what do you think of it Danny"?

Danny pretends to examine it thoroughly, he holds it up to his ear. After a while he says, "Ah now Johney I'm afraid to say you've wasted your money. You can hear plainly she's off the timing, too many ticks and not enough tocks", Johney laughed hearty at this knowing Danny is only joking. "Bring her back to Cassie and demand your money back", said Danny.

Johney was slapping his knee and laughing, "I would Danny but I haven't paid anything yet. The payments don't start to the first of April".

Granny whispers under her breath, "All fool's day". "There is also a rumour going around that yourself and Kitty Meehan are getting married. Still laughing hearty Johney announced, "Your some boyo Danny".

Tess puts Dannys egg on the table she said "Would you stop your hashing and leave poor Johney alone". I only saying what I hear in the country", said Danny. "It's alright Tess" Johney replied.

I know he's only having a bit of fun. Kitty got me to dig up her flower garden, that's all".

"I heard there's more to it than that", insisted Danny. "Who was the swanky car"?

His father cleared his throat. "It's a man from the electric board, going to install electricity for us". After a few moments silence Danny asked, "well what did you tell him?"

"We told him we or nobody else around here would be interested in having electric", said Granny. Danny let a sigh, "why didn't you make him wait until I came back".

"Because it doesn't matter what you'd say", Dan replied, "We are getting no electricity. As well as that what right have you to send in a list of names without asking these people first". We'll not to be tying ourselves down to paying a bill every month".

"But me and Bosco talked it over and we both agreed it's what the country needs. It's the future. "They had installed a couple of years ago in Rathlee and they'd tell you it was the best job they ever done".

His father wasn't giving in "They've better land over there, a more prosperous part of the country". "They're not stuck in the dark ages", answered Danny, "Like we are here".

Granny spoke sharply, "Why don't you listen to your father".

Danny answered back, "I was talking to Andy of the hallow, he said he'd be interested".

Granny sneered, "He would as long as he got some other poor devil to pay the bills".

The discussion continued, Danny claiming it was time to modernise, but his father with help from Granny warning it would come at too hefty a cost.

Again Danny tried, "Me and Bosco……… Dan pulled his chair out and jumped up. He banged his fist of the table. Danny never saw him as angry before. "You and Bosco, the two of you will soon be running the country. Its time you got it into your head as long as I'm boss, I'll say what we can or can't have. You can do what you like when you take over. Last year you were looking for a new bicycle. Then you mentioned a tractor earlier this year, now electricity. What's next? "It's time you pulled in your horns boy"

He nodded at Johney and they both left. Granny rose shuffled to the bedroom, Danny started to eat his breakfast.

As she poured his tea, his mother, quiet all along spoke up. "I'm sorry Danny, but you must understand your father's side. You know money is tight. With careful management we just about get by. For your father, getting by, without going into debt is the only option. I can also see your side where you'd have items that would make life handier but who knows maybe in a few years there might be more money about".

"I suppose your right ma", Danny replied. "It's just Bosco and I talked it over, we decided if we had electricity we could learn to weld, start making gates and feeding troughs, things like that, we could pay for the electricity and have money left over, so that we wouldn't be always begging for money if we were going anywhere".

With breakfast over he started his usual chores, his first job was to bring hay to the bullocks in the back field. He always liked going down to the back field. It ran down to the river. Down there nobody could see him, it was so quiet and peaceful. There was always wild life of some kind down by the river, waterhens, a crane or maybe Jip might come on a rabbit he could chase. He sat down on a large flat stone located behind the hedge. He reflected on the mornings proceedings. Could they not see it was as much for their benefit as his. Granny could have her room properly heated. Lamps wouldn't have to be light and repaired all the time. His mother would have a proper light to do her knitting and sewing. He smiled and thought of the immense job Bosco would have had convincing his father, they needed electricity. Somewhere from the distance he heard his father calling him.

CHAPTER 3

Every evening after the milking was completed granny insisted for the rosary to be said "At least he'll have a bit of religion before he goes out rambling". The rosary was just finished when Edmund Coyle arrived. Edmund was a batchalor of around seventy who lived about a mile from the Higgins. He called over every Tuesday and Friday nights. Dan always called with Edmund on Sunday nights. Even though he was friendly with Edmund, Dan was wary of him, Danny often heard his father say "He's a dangerous man. He thrives on gossip. What's said here one night he'll repeat in some other house the next night and the bigger the scandal the better". Danny wasn't keen on him either for he never had a good word to say about the youth of the neighbourhood. A favourite saying of his was, "A couple of years in the army would straighten them out".

This evening Edmund was beaming. He had a large piece of news to tell the Higgins. A man from the electricity had been going around the houses looking for clients to sign up to take electricity, Edmund had been talking to Andy of the hallow and this man arrived with him this morning. Seemly some young lad had sent them a letter saying there were many interested in electricity in this part of the country. "Andy and myself come to the conclusion it's a good chance it was Owenie Carlin. It would be like something the clown would be at. He sent them a list of all the ones interested".

"Granny spoke up", Is Andy of the hallow signing up"?

He said he might be interested but he'd wait and see what the rest would do", said Edmund. I was then talking to Hugh Gribbons and he told me the man called at several houses and got chased everytime so he didn't go down the road any further".

"What made you think it was Owenie Carlin"?, enquired Danny.

Edmund laughed. "For that's the kind of idiot he is, he would take in hands to govern the whole country. As well as that he has a couple of stuck up sisters. They'd like to be better than anybody else and have everything handy."

"Maybe Martin, who's doing well in England might be paying to have it installed", Danny suggested.

Edmund cut in right away, "Is he doing well? I'd like to see it with my own two eyes before I'd believe it". "I would be suspicious myself", granny agreed.

"Why don't you and granny slip over to London and make enquiries", said Danny, "who knows you could be very surprised".

Bosco just then came through the door. "Just in time Bosco, Edmund and Granny are going to London to find out how Martin Carlin is doing", said Danny.

"I can save them the bother", Bosco replied. "I was talking to his father and he told me he is well, on the way to being a millionaire".

Edmund shook his head. "I wouldn't take his word for anything".

Danny winked over at Bosco. "Is it true your father is interested in having electricity installed"? "Oh! aye I mentioned it to him and he said the sooner the better". "Isn't it wonderful", answered Danny, that there's one forward thinking man in the country".

Tess decided to change the subject "Surely to goodness you two boys are not going out to night again". "Indeed we are Tess", answered Bosco. "We've two classy birds to meet and we wouldn't want a few smart boys wiping our eyes".

"They are lucky girls to have met you two lads", teased Tess. "Lucky is the perfect word", announced Danny. "With our bicycle clips in our pockets and a smell of paraffin oil off us, we are mighty catches, they are probably after our money". Danny headed towards the door "Aye, that the reason alright, come on Bosco let's get going, it would be a calamity if we were late".

"Wait", said Bosco, "I have no bike. Our auld fella was coming home last night, of course he had no lights, hit a pothole and buckled the front wheel".

Danny turned back scratching his head. "Damn it anyway, but hold on, all's not lost. Edmund will lend you his bicycle". Edmund shuffled in the chair. "No chance. As the man says I always abide by the rule, not a borrower or a lender be". "You must take me to be a real fool, to give you my bike, to have some blackguard about the town steal it, not likely".

"I thought that would be the answer", murmured Danny. "You can take mummy's". Bosco looked over at Tess. "Ach, go ahead and take it I wouldn't see you stuck". Tess was delighted to give Edmund a dig.

17

After they left granny got on her high horse "What's going to become of their generation . Run, run, run. It's a mystery why they can't sit in the house at nights.

Edmund continued the discussion "Habit, Mrs Higgins that's what it is, nothing else. Not comparing them to dogs but if a dog forms a habit to ramble he'll never stop. I'm telling you its just the same with humans. In our time Dan ...."

Tess butted in "If only you'd listen to yourselves comparing the lads to rambling dogs, they are from a different generation than you. They have a completely different lifestyle, different concerns, they see things not as you see them, they have new ideas. That's the reason why that young fella, whoever he is, wants to have electricity. He sees it as vital if he going to progress in life and make something of himself but instead of encouraging them your generation want to keep your foot on their throats all the time. Will it work we'll see shortly but I fairly sure it won't" Tess leaves and goes outside she could feel the tears welling up inside as she wandered down the lane. "I just couldn't let that pass", she thought, "and Dan sitting and not saying a word. If we don't speak they think we have the same mindset Ah! Like dogs rambling, how are you"

All went to plan, Danny and Bosco arrived just as the show was about to start. Danny entered, located the two girls and sat down beside Alice. Five minutes later Bosco, who had taken a "loan"out of his sister's piggybank slide into a seat near hand. As the lights brightened at the interval Danny greeted Bosco as if he hadn't seen him for a while. Bosco then moved up beside Danny. Afterwards Danny hinted about treating the girls to chips and the girls agreed. The conversation between Susan and Bosco seemed to flow quite easily. Danny mentioned they'd walk them the half mile home, none of them objected. "A very successful venture", announced Danny as they cycled home. "I think Susan has a liking for you". "And I'd have no bother liking her" Bosco replied. They all agreed to meet up on Tuesday night. "Ach we'll have to make an afford to pay them in", suggested Bosco. "It's time enough for that type of thing", answered Danny. "Anyway where are we going to pick up that kind of cash to be so generous".

Next morning at the crossroads Bosco was on a high. "The more I thought about last night the better I feel about the whole situation. Mammy was still up when I arrived home, so I told her out straight, I'd met a lovely girl and I asked her if she'd like to go to the cinema. I then hinted I'd need some cash. I nearly fell off the chair when she'd agreed with me and promised she see I wasn't stuck for a few bob each week. Rubbing his hands together he announced, "Things are looking up".

CHAPTER 4

"What night are you going to Pat Burke's wake"? asked Granny.

"I was talking to Edmund and we decided we'd go tonight", replied Dan.

Pat Burke was a bachelor farmer who lived about two miles from the Higgins. He hadn't been ailing as far as the neighbours knew but Cathal Green found sitting on a bale of hay in the shed, as Cathal put it, "Dead as Ceasar" This was the big news of the week in the neighbourhood. At Seventy seven a few thought he had a good innings especially as he was out and about, still farming to the last.

"I never heard of him being sick in his life", commented Tess. The Burkes were hardy breed" said Granny.

"Pat had two uncles who lived well into their eighties".

Johney the Spade was eating his breakfast, enjoying his boiled egg and toast. "I done work for him down through the years mostly at the digging of the potatoes. He had fierce good spuds".

"Aye", replied Dan "His land suited the growing of spuds. He supplied Sweeny's shop for years".

"He was always very decent to me", said Johney. "And he seemed pretty well off. I presume he hadn't any brothers or sisters".

"He had two brothers and two sisters", said Dan.

"Is that a fact, I didn't know about them", said Johney.

Granny shuffled in her chair. "One brother James was killed in the quarry he was only twenty, the other one was a good for nothing blaggard. He had a row with the parish priest at the time, Father Lynch, hit him and broke his nose. He fled the country, good riddance. I'm sure Pat never heard from him again. A real vicious hound. One of the sisters was a nun in Dublin and the other one went to England".

Tess seemed anxious to change the subject. "You've got a new spade Johney".

"Ah! No Mrs Higgins it's only a new handle. I was prising a stone at Simpsons a few days ago and the handle let a loud crack. So I got a new shaft put in. It's a good job".

From outside came a whistling sound. Danny was sauntering up the lane. He and Bosco had a longer than usual conversation and it could have even went on a bit longer only Bosco's father let a fierce gulder out of him, warning Bosco if he didn't return home right away he'd come down to the crossroads and beat them black and blue. Both agreed he would and all. "Crabbit bloody man", remarked Bosco. As he sprinted down the road and up lane.

"I don't understand why Bosco puts up with him", thought Danny.

The debate that lenghthened their stay at the crossroads this morning was solely to do with their love lives. Both had run into a bit of bother, Danny's problem was discussed first, as it seemed most serious. A near neighbour of the McAree's, a fella who was a member of Kickhams the parish football team, the same one Danny played on, warned Danny to be very careful because Alice's father was very protective of her and had made it known if he caught young Higgins near his daughter he's leave him he wouldn't be able to walk for a week. They weren't too sure if the threat was real or not because the football fella was known to wind people up.

"I can't take the chance", said Danny. He could leave me in the hospital for weeks".

Bosco let a laugh. "Can you imagine what Edmund and your Granny would say, Alice never said anything about her father not wanting you seeing her".

"I suppose we'll have to be very vigilant", Danny warned. "If I saw him coming I think I'd be able to outrun him".

The conversation dragged on and what ifs were all teased out. "There's that dark lane we pass when we're walking them home if he hid up there and sneaked out behind me, I wouldn't stand a chance", Danny reckoned. "Do you remember the other night Alice was telling us her father spent five or six years in the army when he was young. They teach them to box and wrestle in there".

"And maim the enemy with one whack", joked Bosco. "I think lad your situation is critical. You might better call in Father McManus to negotiate a peace deal with him (mimicking Father McManus) "after hours of talks Daniel we've come to an agreement. Mister McAree has promised to inflict no pain on you if you make a solemn promise not to put a hand on any body part of his loving daughter Alice I sincerely hope you keep your part of the bargain".

Both of them had a laugh and then moved on to discuss Bosco's problem. Bosco had fallen head over heels in love with Susan. Many times he claimed to Danny that she was the most important thing in his life. The problem arose when Susan casually announced to Bosco it was just a month until her birthday. He wasn't too sure if she was dropping a hint about a present or not.

Again the subject was thoroughly discussed. "Well its very simple, it's essential you buy her a present and a danged good one", explained Danny. I'm sure you want this romance to last".

"Certainly I do", replied Bosco. "But where the devil am I going to pick up a pound or so to purchase a present".

"A pound", exclaimed Danny. "What in heavens would you get for a pound. The least you'd have to invest is three pounds".

Bosco let a sigh. "And from where do you think I can gather up three pounds. Mammy gives me the odd bob but it hardly keeps me going. Some weeks she either forgets or she doesn't have it".

Danny spat out onto the ground before he spoke. "I wouldn't fancy having to do it myself but I'm afraid you'll have to approach the auld fella".

"No bloody way", answered Bosco. "I'd be risking my life. I asked him last week for two shillings to buy a tube for the bicycle, he was graiping manure at the time. He swung the graip over my head. "Go and fix the old one you lazy hoor", he shouted. "That was the end of that".

They discussed Bosco's dilemma further then out of the blue Danny had a bright idea.

"Hold on lad all's not lost. Johnny the Spade was in our house a fortnight ago and he had purchased a new pocket watch out of Cassie Byrne's catalogue. The best part of it is he'll have it a month before he has to pay any money and then the cost is spread over 12 months. I think the payment would be around three shillings a month".

"Well it sounds good", agreed Bosco, but what would happen if I wasn't able to keep up the payments "I could help you out", said Danny. "At least Susan wouldn't know who was paying for it. Right we'll go over to Cassie's some evening soon and see what she can offer".

As Danny sauntered down the road he smiled when he thought how worried Bosco was about the birthday present but he thought his problem was much greater and more frightening. He met his father and Johnny coming out the door. "Come on boy and throw the breakfast into you", said Dan. "And hurry out to the wee field for Eddie Finnigan is coming on Friday to plough it and we'd need to have the spuds all lifted out of the pits before then".

Danny greeted Johney. "How's she cutting Johney? What's this I see a new handle in your spade, he takes the spade out of the sack and pretends to examine it.

"What do you think of it? questioned Johney. "A good job isn't it?" Danny shook his head.

"Well to tell you the truth old man, it's not. It's been put in crooked, it's all away to the one side, a real botch job. I suppose it'll have to do now who put it in for you?"

"Willie Rushe, who works in the forge", said Johney. "Danny, I know your only codding". He was laughing to himself as he walked away, "Danny your some boyo".

Danny was still eating his breakfast when the postman, Peter OLoane arrived. As he handed over the letter he remarked. "I suppose you've heard about Pat Burke passing away".

"Indeed we have Peter", answered Tess. "He was a nice quiet type of man".

"Indeed he was all that" replied Peter. "There was never a Christmas passed when he didn't give me something. I know he had a sister living in Manchester for she was home eight or nine years ago. Was there just the two of them"?

Granny spoke up. "There were five of them altogether. There was another girl who became a nun, and there was two other boys. Jim, the oldest was killed in a quarry when he was twenty. Then the other one, Leo, got himself into all kinds of bother including hitting the Parish Priest one time at a dance in the hall and breaking his nose. He was chased out of the Parish after that. Good riddance I'd say. Nobody knows where he went and most don't care". "I never heard of him", said Peter. "But hitting the priest wouldn't have gone down well. I suppose maybe too much drink taken".

"He had none at all" confirmed granny. "What happen was, on Halloween night, he stole an old woman's gate . The wee woman, Kitty Doogan, went looking for it the next morning, found it in a drain about three hundred yards away. She went down to try and lift it out, slipped and hit her head. She was found dead that afternoon".

"Nobody knows for sure who hid the gate", explained Tess.

Granny insisted. "It was him alright, somebody met him on his way home from doing the evil deed. Then the priest confronted at the dance and asked him to leave. He struck him and broke his nose. That was the finish of him around these parts, so he upped and left".

"Maybe it was just a bit of devilment that went wrong", hinted Peter". I know they still do silly things like that around our parts at Halloween".

Danny finished his breakfast. "I never heard that story before and nobody knows where he ended up".

"Now that you mention it I delivered Pat a few air mail letters recently, they could be from him".

Peter left and Danny made his way to the potato field. Tess decided to confront granny about accusing Leo Burke of taking and hiding the gate. "I wish you wouldn't accuse Leo Burke when your not sure if he hid the gate or not".

"Of coarse he done it. As well as that everybody at the dance saw him hit Father Lynch. Edmund Coyle was at the dance that night he told me you could hear the bang two hundred yards away. And as the bucko was going out the door everyone in the hall clapped".

Tess could feel her temper boilover. She threw the dish cloth across the table. "Now I'm going to tell you the truth" she screamed I know for certain Leo did not take Kitty Doogan's gate that night. Then when big brave Father Lynch, thought he'd the backing of the crowd, roared at him to get out of "My hall" imagine his hall, and when Leo asked him why was he ordering him to leave, he shouted at him that he was a murderer and made to strike him but he missed then Leo hit him and sent him flying on his backside into the corner. Then he turned and left. Edmund must have thrived on that scandal for years, but Edmund was right the whole crowd stood and clapped, not because Leo left but because they realised somebody should have done it years before. She banged her fist off the table. "That's what happened that night I was there and THAT'S what happened". She turned and fighting back the tears rushed outside. As she passed the window she could see granny hobble up to her bedroom.

CHAPTER 5

Edmund arrived at eight o'clock to go with Dan to Pat Burkes wake. Dan was putting on his shoes "I'll be ready in a minute Edmund".

Oh! there's no rush, as the man says it's a long time to daylight", joked Edmund. Danny appeared out of his room dressed in his good clothes. "Surely to goodness your not going out tonight", queried Tess". "Your father wanted you to keep an eye on the black cow, he thinks she could calve anytime".

"You know Bosco and I go to the pictures on Tuesday nights", said Danny. "Anyway that cow won't calve for a couple of days yet". Dan cleared his throat "It wouldn't kill you to stay in for one night"

"But as you know Bosco and I are seeing these two wonderful girls", replied Danny. And it has come to a crucial period in our courtships. If we let them slip through our fingers we could end up two cranky old bachelors, I'm taking your bike mam".

Dan was combing his hair "I don't know what the next generation will turn to be".

"There's a lot of foreign influences in Ireland at the minute", replied Edmund. He remembered how annoyed Tess got a few weeks ago so he didn't elaborate any further.

"I suppose there's little chance of Leo appearing", Dan queried.

Edmund let a loud laugh, "I'd be very surprised if he did. I'm sure Pat hasn't been in contact with him since he left. How would he know Pat died as the man says he's as well staying where he is". As Dan moved towards the door Tess said "Tell whoever is in charge down there that I'll go down tomorrow and help out".

Tess was still up when Dan arrived home. He was able to say Cathal Green and the wife seemed to have organised the wake and were delighted Tess had volunteered to help. When Tess questioned if there was any word of Leo Dan said he'd heard someone mention he'd been in contact with Pat for a number of years and indeed Pat telephoned him several times. There was also talk he may attend the funeral. The sister who is a nun in Dublin would only be able to attend the funeral mass and then travel back as requested by her order. His other sister in Manchester was in poor health and wouldn't attend. She never married.

On the way home when Dan brought up the subject of Pat being in touch with Leo, Edmund went deadly quiet. "I mentioned it several times", said Dan, but he didn't comment That man would get better mileage out of the story if there was still friction between Pat and Leo".

CHAPTER 6

As they cycled home, after walking the girls home, Danny had an inkling Bosco was anxious about something. It turned out Susan informed him her birthday was just three weeks away. Bosco had innocently said, "I suppose I'd better have a present for you". Susan give his arm a squeeze. "You'd better", she commented. "Three blinking weeks and I haven't done anything about it yet and I know she was deadly in earnest".

"Don't panic", said Danny. "We'll visit Cassie Byrne some evening this week, you can pick something and it'll arrive in 10 days or so. Your love life will be saved".

"She brought up another subject lately. As you knew since her father died four years ago, they have no man about the house, her mother was wondering if I would do some digging in the garden".

Danny burst out laughing "They're starting to reel you in man, once the mother becomes involved your about to lose your freedom. What did you tell her"?

"I told her it was busy time of the year on the farm but when the days grew longer I might be able to do a few hours. I was thinking if I can keep her mother happy it would be a great feather in my cap". The conversation lasted all the way home.

Bosco was now seeing Susan on Friday nights as well as Tuesday nights. "You see the mother and Christina, Susan's Sister, the only one at home, goes to visit Susan's granny and doesn't appear back to eleven o clock. I've left by then". "Bloody good arrangement" commented Danny. "Aye, and the best of all is, there's no cost to it", said Bosco. "And she has always something fancy to eat." Bosco then quizzed Danny on how his relationship with Alice was progressing Danny assured him, he wasn't near as keen on Alice as he was with Susan "With football training and going over to St Joseph's hall in Killgubbin to the dance on a Sunday nights I'm happy with just a Tuesday night. As well I think were too young to settle down".

Bosco disagreed. "I think Susan and I was made for each other". As they reached the cross roads Danny mentioned that they should travel down to Cassie Bryne's the next evening. "We'll agree a time in the morning but of coarse you might be in Susan's garden, digging like crazy. Oh! aye, and another thought has come to me If you would need some help at it I'm sure your auld fella will help you out".

As Bosco threw his leg over the bicycle he shouted back. "You're some bloody help".

CHAPTER 7

Next day Tess wrapped some scones she had baked, put them in a wicker basket and cycled down to Burkes. She was met by Mrs Green and then made her way up to where the corpse lay in the bedroom, said her prayers and then joined Mrs Green and another woman in the kitchen. Mrs Green commented there was a few coming and going but no big rush. Tess announced she could stay a few hours if any of them needed a break they could go home. Mrs Green said she wasn't long there but the other woman said she'd go home and come back later on when no doubt things would be busier.

A wake where there's no near relations involved usually is not as sombre as one where a partner or offspring are there. This was the case at Pats wake and Tess and Mrs Green were enjoying each others company. Mrs Green explained to Tess how they come to live a few hundred yards past Pats house. Cathal and her met in England and they both yearned to come back home and buy a small farm, which they could work while still holding down two jobs. They were delighted at their purchase and also to have the good luck to have such a lovely neighbour in Pat.

Tess was there about an hour and a half, filling kettles, making sandwiches when a noise of a motor filled the air and McClements taxi from the town appeared. Tess peered out through the kitchen door and saw a fairly large distinguished looking man disembark, he stood looking round and Tess immediately sensed it was Leo.

"Quick quick," she said to Mrs Green. "You go out and meet that stranger for I think its Leo and he'll want to hear all details of Pats death". Mrs Green took off her apron, give her hair a brush and was just in time to meet the stranger at the living room door. With the door open a few inches Tess could clearly hear the conservation and she was right it was Leo. She heard him tell Mrs Green, Pat seemed to have reasons to believe this would be the way he'd go. In a fairly strong American drawl he told Mrs Green he had spoken to him on the phone three months previous and he said if anything happened to him he'd leave his number with Fr McManus to ring him and Fr McManus rang him yesterday with the sad news.

Mrs Green escorted Leo up to the bedroom and almost instantly Tess's heart started pounding. "What should she do"? she thought, pretend she didn't remember him or maybe slip out and leave but that wouldn't be fair as she was now the only one in the kitchen. "Play it by ear", she whispered to herself.

Leo and Mrs Green seemed along time up in the room. Two women and a man rose and left the house empty. Tess kept busy. Then she heard the two come down from the room. Mrs Green told Leo to have a seat and she would get him some tea.

She then came in and says to Tess "Go you out and chat to Leo I'm sure you remember him". She fixed her hair and went into the living room. Leo was looking all around the room. "Leo", said Tess. Leo turned around to see who was there, "Hello", he replied. "Oh my god it's you Tess", he jumped up, shook her hand and kissed her on the cheek" Oh! Tess it's so good to see you after all these years and your looking fabulous".

Tess could feel herself blushing. "Your standing the times well yourself Leo".

"Sit down Tess" said Leo "there's so much I have to ask". "And me too", Tess answered. "I suppose I know a little bit more about you than you do about me", said Leo. "I have been in touch with Pat this last seven or eight years and he told me a few things about you, how you married Dan Higgins and had one son, a fine lad Pat said."

"You may tell me a bit about what you've been up to since", said Tess, "for most of the neighbours had you dead".

Leo laughed hearty at that. Then he told Tess he'd worked a while in Dublin and then travelled to New York. After a few years working in construction he was accepted into the police force. "Imagine that", he laughed. "Me the big bad beast that clabbered the parish priest was now keeping law and order on the streets of New York". Mrs Green came in with tea and Leo told Tess about his marriage to a girl from Toronto. They have two girls, both doing well for themselves.

"Emma my youngest is flying in tomorrow morning for the funeral", "she intends to stay a few days so I'm sure you'll meet her. She's twenty eight".

Mrs Green came in and told Tess that another neighbour had now taken up residence in the kitchen and if she felt the need to go home they were blessed with plenty of help now.

"Well seeing I'm only sitting in the way I'd be better anywhere", said Tess with a laugh. She put on her coat and prepared to leave. Leo rose from the chair. "I'll walk you to the end of the lane". It's quite a while since I walked a pretty colleen down a country lane." Thirty six years last November", answered Tess.

"My god, exclaimed Leo, you've that figure well established in your head". "You can say that again", replied Tess.

They walked a while in silence then Leo stopped took Tess hand. "Look Tess I owe you a big apology, when I left I promised I'd keep in touch, but my head was all over the place. My two sisters said they didn't want to ever see me again, that I shamed the Burke name. I wrote once after I settled in New York and Kathleen replied telling me never to write again. So I didn't. Three years later my mother passed away and they didn't let me know. Can you imagine your mother dying and no one telling you just because I stood up against a bully who was telling lies and untruthful rumours about me". They walked slowly on "You know well it wasn't me who took off kitty Doogan's gate and threw it in the drain" continued Leo.

"Off coarse I knew", replied Tess, "and it was hard to listen to all those lies and rumours then and down through the years since even to this very day knowing that they weren't true because we'd spent that evening together down at the crooked bridge".

They walked another bit in silence. Then Leo said, "Do you remember that night Tess, a bright moon shone down and we dandered along until we came to the bridge. There was a noise of splashing and I knew it was a salmon I wanted to go down and take a look but you coaxed me not to. "Let the poor thing alone you said".

"I complained I was cold", Tess added. "And you took off your jacket and made me wear it. I don't think I was ever as happy as that night Leo".

"Yes I was pretty happy myself" Leo replied and to think there wouldn't be any more like it. I repeated it in my head many many times in those first few years". I was looking forward to other evenings like it but ……….. . The ironic thing about all of that trouble was I knew from day one who took off that poor woman's gate".

Tess seemed surprised. "Did you"? "Yes you see when I was making my way home after we went our ways from the scyamores. I heard voices coming in the opposite direction so I stood in the shadows of a large tree until they passed by. I knew one of them by his squeaky voice, a small red haired guy from near Killgrubbin called Colm OSullivan. I didn't recognise the other lad. They were laughing about removing several gates and Kitty Doogan's was one they mentioned".

"You never said anything to me", said Tess.

"No Tess I didn't, I knew the lads meant no harm, it was a bit of devilment unfortunately went wrong. You see if I'd told you sometime through the years it would have been normal for you to tell the whole story. I'm sorry but I wouldn't have liked getting those guys in trouble".

Tess let a giggle. "That was always your problem Leo you were too soft".

Leo changed the subject "Tess how has your life been. Was it a happy one"?

Tess started to tie the belt of her coat. "I have made it this far without any more upheavel in my life. I waited every day, for weeks, month's aye years for the promised letter. Now I didn't become a recluse. I worked in Morgan's the general merchants, danced, mostly on Sunday nights. A few lads brought me to the pictures but nothing serious developed. Dan was always in the shop buying feeding stuffs and things for the farm and I enjoyed his company, platonic like. Then out of the blue he asked me if I'd like to try a new restaurant that had opened in Glenbrack. Can you imagine, some lad asking me out to a restaurant over twenty years ago, I accepted and our relationship grew. He was trustworthy and kind and I was now over thirty. There's no getting away from it, passion was light on the ground. But even though he was fourteen years older than me when he asked me would I marry him it seemed the right option. Less than a year later Danny was born. His mother lives with us".

"She's still living: she must be quite old now", said Leo. "She's in her nineth year", said Tess. "How do you get on with her"? queried Leo.

"Ninety percent of the time alright but the other ten she can try my patience. So that's it we plod along making ends meet".

She then asked Leo about his life. He told that he now lives upstate New York, retired from the police force but still has a part-time job with a security firm. His wife Jane does quite a bit of travelling due to her job as a fashion designer. They arrived at the bottom of the lane where Tess's bicycle lay against the bank.

"This is my mode of transport", said Tess. "It was nice seeing you again after all this time. I'd given up hope along time ago of ever meeting you again".

"Yes, I'm delighted to have met you", answered Leo. I'll be hanging about for a few days, Emma and I, so maybe we can get together again. I'd like to meet Danny" "Well why not", answered Tess. "Why don't call up some day. Nobody will bite you because no one knew all those years ago, I had anything to do with the ruffian of the parish".

"I'll just do that", Leo agreed, and please please again accept my apology. I'm so sorry that I broke my promise to you". He give her a kiss on the cheek and sauntered back up the lane again.

As she cycled the road home Tess reflected on her youth and the crush she had on Leo. He was her first real boyfriend but they kept their romance a secret from their family and friends mostly because she was only sixteen and he was twenty three. They had a spot where they used to meet behind some scyamore trees. Many times in the two years ahead they talked about the future. Leo said when she was older around nineteen they'd emigrate to England, but she'd just turned eighteen when the episode with Father Lynch took place. The Monday night after Tess went as usual to "their" special place Leo was already there waiting on her. It was there he said he'd have to leave, everybody of his parents generation was horrified at him hitting the priest. "I'll write to you in a week or so and we can arrange to meet", said Leo. Her whole worry was that it would come when she was at work and her mother would open it. She met the postman most mornings as he started his rounds. So one morning she asked him if he had a letter for her could he drop it into Morgans shop, the letter never came. Maybe it was all for luck she thought although at the time it blighted a large part of her life.

CHAPTER 8

The next morning they decided to visit Cassie Byrnes that evening. They'd meet at the crossroads around eight o'clock.

"It'll be dark when we arrive down there" said Bosco "for I wouldn't want anyone seeing us there" "Why not"? questioned Danny.

"Because if she would lose money in this venture of hers people would say I didn't pay her for what I ordered" said Bosco.

Danny kicked a stone down the road. "For godsake grow up, you're a courting man now not a school boy you shouldn't worry about what people say. See you tonight here at eight oclock".

When Danny arrived Bosco was already there. "Wait to you see came in the post this morning" said Bosco taking an envelope from his pocket and handing it to Danny.

Danny took the letter from the envelope and went to the end of it to see who had sent it. "Martin bloody Carlin", Danny exclaimed. "He must be looking for something"

Bosco spat on the ground "He doesn't have to look for anything the blinking man has all he wants" Bosco let

Danny finish reading the letter. "What do you think of that? He's working twelve hours a day, when he was at home the mother could never get him up before dinner time. "What a change around".

Danny shook his head "Look at his wages, eighteen pounds a week, that's over three times a good trades man earns here. How long has he been away? Eighteen months if that".

Bosco takes the letter from Danny and reads "I'm saving hard and hope by the end of this year I'll have enough cash to buy a pub. My local at the minute is owned by a Wexford bloke, he's thinking of selling it and he is giving me first offer of it, but then I give him a fair amount of cash at the weekends. It's all brandy I drink now, I don't suppose you have started on the alcohol yet".

Bosco folds the letter "Your dead right Martin, I haven't started drinking alcohol if I could raise the cash to buy an orange crush to wash down my chips on a Tuesday I'd be delighted".

"Give me that letter again Bosco". Danny opens it and reads "How is Danny getting on? I suppose he's still going out with the wee McAree girl. Not a bad girl, plain looking and not much passion in her". Danny let a grunt. "He'd say that wouldn't he just because I wiped his eye away back. He never forgave me." He reads more "I suppose he's still trying to play football. I don't know how he can be bothered running through muck every Sunday after a ball and getting belted up the mouth every so often". He folds the letter and hands it back to Bosco.

As they made their way to Cassie's they discussed Martin and his letter. Danny asked Bosco was he thinking of answering it. "I'll probably send him a few lines but it'll not be all truth I'll be telling him!

"Aye that's a good idea, tell him a pack of lies. Tell him Alice and I got engaged and I'm now the star player on the football team and there's talk it won't be long until I'm on the County team".

Bosco laughed. "I'll tell him Pat Burkes farm is up for sale and I hope to buy it".

Do you know what you should tell him Bosco? That you've invested your money in fine jewellery"

"I will not", replied Bosco. "I might have to ask him to help me out with the payments".

"He's no word of coming home", Danny remarked, "but I suppose with working long hours drinking brandy and buying property he wouldn't have time to visit a rundown place like this".

Cassie Byrne was a pleasant woman of around fifty. It was a great surprise in the neighbourhood when she had started such an enterprise. She had no experience in the retail trade and many predicted if she wasn't careful there was smart guys about, who'd take advantage of her. When they arrived the only person there was a middle aged man, which none of them knew, giving Cassie an order for two pipes.

With his business completed he turned around and began to laugh "I bet these lads are looking for presents for their girlfriends. You've come to the right place. That catalogue is full of wonderful items that any girl would want. (whispering) There's plenty of nice underwear, always a favourite with the ladies".

"It's something for ourselves", Danny lied. Cassie seemed embarrassed by the mentions of underwear and ushered the man towards the door. "That's a great auld idiot" said Cassie "I'll give you a catalogue and you can browse over it in your own time. I'm taking a cup of tea for I've been very busy all evening".

She offered them tea but both declined. They flicked through the crowded pages. They both agreed it was hard to single out one item to purchase, taking into consideration of his finances Bosco plumped for a bracelet at two pounds and six shillings.

Cassie then worked out the monthly payments. "Four shillings and two pence is the damage" she said "I'll have it ready for collection in ten days time. You can call for it or I can deliver it if you want".

"Oh not at all", answered Bosco. "I'll call for it".

As they rode home they discussed this new service, Cassie was providing. "There's a lot of stuff in that book", maintained Bosco. "What do you think of your man suggesting the underwear"?

"It would be hard to know how she'd take it", said Danny. "If her mother took it the wrong way Father McManus could be giving you a call (mimicking Father McManus) Mr and Mrs McNamee your son Bosco has been purchasing underwear, wee lacy things for his girlfriend and then he insisted seeing her wearing them just to be sure they fitted well"

"Either Father McManus or myself would probably receive a hefty boot up the backside from the auld fella".

Bosco's whole worry now was finding the four shillings and two pence each month.

"You'll just have to manage your finances better", Danny commented. "Cut back on luxuries".

"Luxuries, what the hell luxuries have I to cut back on, pictures once a week and a bobs worth of chips afterwards. How could I cut back on that"? Danny laughed.

"I must admit it seems almost impossible".

CHAPTER 9

Two days after Pat Burkes funeral as they were having their breakfast, there was a knock on the door and when Tess opened it Leo and his daughter were standing there. Emma was a very pretty girl and when Tess introduced them all to Leo and Emma. Danny felt slightly embarrassed. It wasn't everyday he met a pretty girl from another country. Leo and Dan fell deep into conversation. Leo was keen to know how the neighbourhood had changed, who had passed away or moved out. Even Granny was pleasant and complimented Leo in having such a beautiful girl.

"There's another one almost identical at home", Leo informed them. "Unfortunately she's away on business with her mother".

"I suppose Pats farm will be sold now", asked Dan.

"Well we haven't made up their minds yet. Emma loves the place but I don't think she'd suit full time farming" joked Leo, but we'll keep it for a while and see how things turns out". Leo then pointed out until the stock is sold they have a problem. Cathal Green who'd taken care of them during Pats wake wasn't about owing to his job. "Danny can keep an eye on them" suggested Tess. "Isn't that right Dan?"

Aye there's no reason why he can't run over and take a look at them, he's usually running other places less important"

Leo informed them he was going back the next day but Emma would be staying to sort out Pats affairs "Danny, you can give her a few agricultural lessons". After they left, Granny announced Leo seemed done well for himself.

Tess poking the fire spoke loud enough to be heard "I had no doubt he would".

The next morning Danny met Bosco at the crossroads, after explaining his new role he added that Leo's daughter was staying a while. "Ah jaysus you'd want to see her", said Danny, "A real beauty, there's no lassie in the parish as good looking as her and no way shy either"

"Is she going to be staying in Pats house"? asked Bosco.

"No, she'll be staying in Powers Hotel in Glenbrack but she says she's looking forward to walking around the whole farm"

"I bet you she doesn't come near the place", replied Bosco, trying to put a damper on the whole proceedings.

"Well anyway I'll be missing from the crossroads in the mornings for a few weeks and there's a chance I'll have to curtail my hectic love life as well", warned Danny. "A man can't serve two masters you know".

Next morning after breakfast Danny cycled over to Pats and met Cathal Green who explained what had to be done. Pat had twelve cows and each one suckled a calf. He had eighteen sheep but neither the cattle or sheep needed feeding. The only stock which had to be fed was the hens and ducks. For the next couple of days Danny travelled over every morning and again in the evening. Three days passed and he never encountered anyone about the place. He was beginning to wonder had Emma already gone back to the States, but on the fourth evening she was there waiting on him. At first Danny was slightly awkward around her. After all she was about ten years older than him and a woman of the world.

"How's the animals getting on"? she asked.

"Fine, they're no bother at all", answered Danny.

"I called out yesterday in the middle of the day but I couldn't stay I had to meet the lawyer after lunch". "Isn't this a glorious place", she said. "I love everything about it, the different noises, faraway dogs barking, wild birds singing, the hens cackling and then the silence. Just to stand here and look around the countryside and appreciate the silence". "Come on", she said. "I'm coming with you on your rounds this evening. "I searched about and found a pair of Pats rubber boots. They're miles too big for me but at least they'll keep my feet dry. There's so much I wish to know about the animals".

They both headed out the back lane to where the livestock were. As Emma asked questions about the beasts, Danny began to feel at ease with her. She seemed so genuine and anxious to learn.

Danny explained to her that all the cows and calves were Aberdeen Angus. "They suit this type of land", he explained. We have the same type and Daddy wouldn't keep any other breed".

Again when they visited the field with the sheep Emma was amused that they all came running to them jostling to get close but Danny explained Pat was probably still giving them meal and that was why they were so friendly. With it being May now said Danny they have plenty of grass and don't need feeding any more. When they come back to the farm yard Danny informed Emma that he'd feed then hens and ducks and gather the eggs from the nests in the hen house.

"This is without doubt the best evening of my life", said Emma. "It's so different to what I'd usually be doing in New York so, so, pleasant and calm".

"How long do you intend to stay"? asked Danny.

"Well I did intend to head back after five or six days but I may delay it a bit longer. I walked the four mile out here this afternoon and I came on Pats bicycle and I cycled down the lane a couple of times until I was confident and I'm riding it back to the hotel this evening and cycle out tomorrow again".

"Right then", said Danny. "I'll call at the about the same time tomorrow evening and I'll give you a few more lessons on farming and the countryside".

"I'll be so much looking forward to that. I'd like to go out as far as Pats farm goes and I'll have plenty of questions to ask".

On his way home Danny once again thought about how well they got on together. It was all so natural and he was surprised he was so comfortable in her company. After all he thought again a stunning girl from a different environment much more mature than he was and they'd hit it off and it was all owing to her attitude. Every evening for the next fortnight, Danny cycled down to Pats after he had the chores cleared up at home. The weather was fine and dry and with the evening lengthening coming towards to the end of May the fields were drying up and turning green again.

Every evening Emma would be waiting, togged out in Pats wellingtons and a jacket away they'd go and inspect the stock. Then Danny would suggest where they should walk Emma was always keen to let Danny know whatever he planned was fine with her. Pats farm was long and narrow so to reach the march ditch it would have been a mile long. Every evening they took a different route, sauntering along, Emma asking questions about different species of trees or birds they came upon along the way. In one corner of a sheltered field, rabbits were feeding on grass and Danny and Emma stood still and watched them.

"Such a fantastic sight", whispered Emma. "Do they not see us or do they know we are no threat to them"?

"They are no length from their burrows and they know they'll be safely in before we would get their length" answered Danny. Danny noticed that on the way back to the house Emma at some point took his hand, maybe going through a rough gap or if they had to climb over a sheugh, and mostly she didn't let go until they were back at the house. After the first day or so she brought some milk and some buns and made tea. There was still food, tea and sugar left over from the wake.

Every evening they sat in the twilight and conversed on everything under the sun, Emma spoke at length about being raised and schooled in New York City and how they moved upstate after her father had retired. She explained that her mother was completely different in character than her father

"He's so much more laid back then mam", she explained. "Mam works for a fashion house and has always critical deadlines to meet. My Sister is exactly the same while I'm more like Daddy". With dusk closing in they'd lock the house up and head off in different directions. "See you tomorrow", Emma would shout as she cycled down the hill from Pats lane.

Their relationship occupied Danny's mind most of the journey home. Even though he was comfortable in her company and looked forward to seeing her every evening when their conversation covered all subjects, he could never imagine their relationship blossoming into something more serious.

"With her being ten years older and in a more mature place", he thought, "it would be up to her to make the first move if she wanted to develop their relationship further".

CHAPTER 10

"Alice isn't happy with you meeting that Yankee one every evening" announced Bosco one of the mornings they met at the crossroads. "I wouldn't be surprised if she ended the relationship with you".

Danny kicked a stone down the road, "It's up to you to assure her it's only for another week or so. The stock will be sold and she'll be leaving again and all will return to normal".

"Well I'd say a week is the longest she'll stick this situation, then she'll tell you to buzz off. As well it's affecting my friendship with Susan. I'm about to give her her birthday present and if we'd happen to spilt up before that, I'd be left paying Cassie Byrne for something that's no good to me".

"Don't worry I'll take it off your hands for about half what you paid for it, it would be ideal for Alice at Christmas", joked Danny. Bosco probed Danny, trying to find out what kind of friendship was between himself and Emma, but Danny kept the details vague.

"What, for instance do you talk about"? asked Bosco,

"Everything under the sun. She was telling me yesterday evening about what men expects from girls in America and let me tell you it would be more advanced than what you'd get from a girl here", lied Danny. "Another day she told me she had developed an urge to marry a Irishman. One evening there was no sign of her when I arrived over but soon she appeared. She had been sunbathing topless in the garden behind the hayshed. She asked me to clasp her bra and pull up the zip on her dress, real casual like".

"Ah go to hell, you're having me on", replied Bosco.

"Indeed I'm not, you must remember Americans are miles ahead of us being forward like that".

"I don't think Susan or Alice will be asking us anytime soon to clip their bras said Bosco. "Last week we were cuddled up on the sofa on Friday night. I managed my hand about four inches above Susan's knee when all of a sudden she snapped her knees shut, damned nearly broke a couple of my fingers".

After he left Bosco Danny had a great laugh at the yarn he'd spun him. The following day his father sent Danny into the village for some nails. He'd just finished his business when he received a dig of a fist in his back. He spun round, who was behind him only Alice's father Paul McAree. Danny nearly fainted. He was seeing Alice off and on for two years or so and they'd been going to the cinema every Tuesday nights for about six months. Himself and Bosco were careful when they left the girls home. They never went any further than he speed limit sign which was around two hundred yards from their houses.

"We'd probably be able to outrun them if they'd happen to come after us but it's hard to know what tactic they'd use to trap us", said Danny. "I know for sure Alice's auld fella can be a vicious bugger". Now Danny was being confronted full on by him.

Paul McAree took a long pull of his cigarette. "You're young Higgins aren't you"? Danny croaked "Aye" not knowing what was coming next "It's you who been seeing our Alice" Dannys throat had dried up and his only reaction to the question was a slight nod.

"What's this story about you two-timing her? Your seeing some American tart that's here, living near you".

"But I'm only looking after her uncle's cattle because he died" pleaded Danny. "There's nothing going on between us".

"I would hope not" continued Paul because thon lassie of our is pretty upset and weepy this last while and her mother and myself wouldn't like to see her treated badly by some smartass. She an innocent wee girl and she seems to having a liking for you".

"I'll not harm her in any way" Danny insisted "Emma, the American will be leaving next week again so things will be back to normal".

Paul stubbed his cigarette out. "Good enough I don't want to have to intervene, why don't you come up to the house some night and not be standing about the roads, we don't bite you know".

As he cycled home Danny could see this whole situation was getting more complicated, instead of the McAree's not wanting him seeing Alice they in fact seemed intent that they'd become an item. The next morning he was waiting before he went over to Pats farm until Bosco arrived, to tell him about his run in with Alice's father.

Bosco listened to the whole story before he commented "You got away handy enough, I know for sure she was annoyed about the Yank. She reckoned it wasn't looking after a few cows which kept you away for a fortnight".

"Do you know something Bosco this last week or so I've sort of gone off Alice. She's so much immature compared to Emma and now I've promised her father I'll call up to the house. What happens if I call the whole affair off?

Bosco giggled, "Not my problem, sir, I'm so happy with my wee Susan. I think we'll be together for a long time. How much longer will Emma be here"?

I think the auction could be in a week or ten days, then she's gone.

CHAPTER 11

When Danny met up with Emma that evening she confirmed that the auction would indeed be in ten day's time "I'll have all his affairs with the lawyer sorted out as well and so I'll be free to travel home".

"You'll be glad to get your life back to normal", commented Danny.

Emma didn't speak for a moment but put her arm inside Danny's. "I've reminded you several times, this has been the best time of my life. Alright I lost my Uncle Pat whom I didn't know well but these evenings with you have been such a pleasure, thanks Danny".

With the auction now advertised in the local papers Danny told Emma he'd spend a few days arranging the items for sale so as to make it easy for the auctioneer and potential purchasers. Apart from the stock there wasn't much else to auction. Pat didn't have a tractor, so apart from turf barrows, milk cans, farm implements and some bales of hay left over from the winter, there wasn't much else.

"I'll leave the house the way it is", said Emma. I'll pack up all the delph and wrap up the bed linen and put it in the top bedroom it would seem the driest room, I hope to come back each summer for a while at least. I'm leaving any of his good clothes in the charity shop and I'm donating his bicycle to you".

"Thanks very much, it's very decent of you", said Danny.

Emma laughed. "It's easy being decent with other folks belongings. "Anyway when I come back next year I'll want to see it to make sure your taking good care of it". If there's any of the tools you or your father would like, take them before the auction day"

"There's nothing we need for", said Danny. "But I see a brand new spade in the turf shed and I wonder could I take it to give to someone who'll appreciate it, he's called Johnny the Spade, his right name is John Brennan but Johnny the Spade is all he gets. His main occupation is making drains for farmers and he thinks more of his spade than quite a few of men thinks of their wives, a bit on the simple side but a gentle soul".

"Done deal", said Emma. I think I remember that man at the wake, "not too well dressed"

"Aye that would be him", Danny replied. "There's lots of smart farmers who take advantage of him, employs him but pays him very little. He's done work for Pat here and he said on the day after Pat died he was one of the most decent men he ever worked for".

"I'll tell you what I'll do", remarked Emma. "I parcel up some of Pats clothes and shoes and you can give them to him as well".

Danny kept the spade and the bundle of clothes in Pats kitchen. One evening he happened to overtake Johnny as he cycled to Pats and told him of his new found wealth. As he put the parcel under his arm and Pats spade in the hessian bag with his own, he continued to thank Emma. As both of them watched Johnny stride down the lane they agreed he seemed to be six inches taller.

"What a nice man", commented Emma, "a proper gentleman. If he was about New York or any big city he would be deceased long ago, robbed and killed".

The evenings up to the day of the auction were fairly busy. Danny and Emma placed somethings around the yard and found that there was much more items than they first believed. Then about two days before the auction the auctioneers clerk came round and numbered each item and logged them.

On the day of the auction a fairly large crowd gathered "Your blessed with this good weather", commented the auctioneer. "It leaves people in a better mood for purchasing".

When the auction ended and purchasers headed off with their new property Emma took hold of Danny's arm "It's pretty sad how it ends up, all the wee important items that Pat would have cherished his pitchforks, rakes and sprayers all gone, spread over the country".

"Well that's it done and dusted", said Danny. "I suppose there's no need for me to come down in the evenings".

"If you don't want to", answered Emma. "But Ive three more days before I go back why don't we meet as usual, I'm sure I'll find some small jobs to do, "I'd be delighted", said Danny. "I'll see you tomorrow as usual".

As he cycled home Danny thought again about the last three weeks. It was a wonderful experience, it also began to dawn on him that he might suffer from withdrawal symptoms when it all ended. He would have been happy if his relationship with Emma could be furthered but there was no use thinking that way because he hadn't a clue what her take on their friendship was.

The next evening when he went to leave, granny piped up "Where are you running to now since the stock are all gone".

Danny thought for a moment "Emma has a few things she wants done before she leaves".

Tess let a giggle "Who knows she might take you back to America with her".

Every evening Emma was ready waiting for him, as usual they dandered along at their leisure stopping now and then to watch the busy birds going back and forth feeding their young or the rabbits blissfully playing in the incline at the foot of the back field.

Once Emma surprised Danny, "Tell me Danny", she asked. "What are your ambitions in life?"

It was something Danny had never thought about. Still only eighteen he assumed he was too young to give it much thought. "I suppose I probably take the same road as my father", "I'll, in a couple of years take over running the farm from my father although I think that'll be a while yet. There's a good chance somewhere along the line I'll find a girl to marry".

They had their arms linked as they walked along she pulled him a little closer and whispered "I hope you do and I hope you'll be always happy".

Emma broke a twig she'd plucked from the hedge "I don't know where I should tell you this or not or maybe you already know but your mother was my father's girlfriend before he left this country". "What! "are you sure"? asked Danny. "I often heard people saying your father was a wild lad when he was younger".

"Yes he was", Emma replied. "He told me himself. The priest of the day accused him in the wrong so he hit him a punch, something that was frowned upon back then. His family disowned him and there wasn't anything else for it but leave. He promised he'd write to your mother but for one reason or another he didn't"

Danny didn't speak for a few seconds. "I never heard my mother mention his name, but come to think of it she always defended him when granny and another neighbour Edmund Coyle would resurrect the incident with the priest every so often".

Emma let a giggle. "Funny, only for that mishap you and I could have been brother and sister".

One evening Emma produced a penknife, she'd found in Pats jacket pocket, "Here Danny carve our initials on a tree so every time I arrive here you and I can come and see them again. It could turn out like a yearly pilgrimage". Danny found a fresh ash tree and carved their initials EB DH. "Put them inside a heart", urged Emma.

When Danny had the task completed Emma took the knife "I'll complete it now" she then carved an L between the initials "Looks well, I wonder what we'll think of it in the future" commented Danny. They both had a good laugh as they moved on.

"Well tomorrow is exist day", said Emma.

There seemed to be an awkward silence between them both realising this was the last walk together "Danny could you meet me tomorrow morning at ten, McClements taxi is leaving me at the airport. I want to give you the key so you can check out the house every so often".

"Ok, I'll be here alright", said Danny, wondering why she couldn't give it to him as soon as she locked up. As they had done every evening they walked down the lane saying their goodbyes as the cycled of in different directions.

The next morning he wasn't too sure how he would approach his father to tell him about having to meet Emma at ten o'clock for he knew they would be going back to the bog to clamping the finish of the turf before the rain would arrive, he struck on a plan. He decided to confide in his mother and ask her for a favour "Ma Emma is leaving at ten o clock for the airport and she wants me to meet her at Pats to give me the key so I can take an odd look into the house".

Tess smiled "Of course. I know your father and you are for the bog but I'll tell him you're doing a message for me and that you'll be along later".

"Thanks ma", said Danny. "She said she didn't want to be like her auld fella, leave and not say goodbye". Tess stopped what she was doing, "So she told you".

"The small bit she knew", said Danny. "Aye" answered Tess "maybe that was enough".

Danny arrived early at Pats house. He felt a strange feeling in his stomach, the last three weeks were the best time he ever had. Again he thought about going back to his old life style but at the moment he didn't want to dwell on it. The taxi chugged up the lane and Emma got out and the car continued up to the turning place. Emma look stunning it was the first time Danny saw her wearing make-up and jewellery, she unlocked the door and ushered Danny into the house, Danny noticed she wasn't as bubbly as before.

"First of all" she said "there's a few pounds in this envelope for all the help you gave us. I don't know how I would have coped without you",

"Ach you shouldn't Emma", Danny argued. "Pats bike is in a garage at the hotel" explained Emma "I told them you would lift it in a day or so if for any reason you spend money on the house just let me know. I'll drop you a note when I arrive home and give you my address. My plans are to come back here next summer".

"I'll keep this place in good shape" Danny assured her "and I will look forward in seeing you again".

"Danny I don't know where you realised it or not but these last few weeks has been such a pleasure and I'm so sad they've ended. If you decide to come over to the States just let me know and I'll arrange to look after you".

"I'll keep that in mind", answered Danny.

Suddenly she throw her arms around Danny's neck catching him unawares pulled him close against her and gave him a long passionate kiss. To Danny it seemed to last for ages, he could smell the delicate aroma of her perfume. She drew away from him a small bit but right away tightened her hold around his neck and kissed him again longer and harder Danny took a while to realise what was happening. He never had been in this situation before. "What was this all about? he thought. His head was in a spin, as Emma pulled away Danny noticed she was crying, should he say something. He wanted to say something, he wanted to tell her he'd fallen in love with her but before he could find the word to say she was in the taxi drying away her tears, almost immediately the engine came to life and the car gently moved away. Emma didn't look back.

Danny wanted to roar at the top of his voice for the car to stop. He had so many questions to ask, maybe he thought Emma would make the taxi driver stop, maybe she had questions to ask aswell. He watched as the car turned right at the end of the lane and crept up the hill. Every second the car was going further away, STOP! STOP! What was that all about Emma. Is there any chance you do love me? He listened as the noise of the engine faded, he stood alone for a long while. A terrible lonely feeling rose up inside him, a feeling he knew would engulf him for a long time. He locked the door and made his way down the lane, he felt rotten. He didn't want to go home to do mundane tasks like clamping turf. When he was near the foot of the lane he remembered the envelope Emma had given him. He opened it to find twenty five pounds and a note.

"Dearest Danny

I don't really know what to say only its breaking my heart to go home. Ive had such a wonderful time and its all because of you. I could easily fall in love with you. The feeling I've felt this last while is so good I really wanted it to last. Bye for now and I can say for certain you'll never be far from my thoughts, Love Emma XXX.

He read it again and again, it answered a few of the questions he wanted to ask but there was still a few others. A cyclist came riding down the hill and made a comment about the weather but Danny barely noticed. He walked up the hill still trying to make sense of what just happened. The rain that had threatened all morning had arrived. Danny thought it was ironic the rain came with perfect timing to sadden the situation further. At the top of the hill he came in line with the march ditch where he and Emma had sauntered along several times in the last three weeks and he couldn't hold back the tears any longer. He cried like he never had before. A sort of hopelessness engulfed him. As he eventually dried his eyes he thought I must get a grip on myself. I have to go home and face the rest and act as nothing has happened.

Jip the dog met him at the foot of the lane, tail wagging, wanting a pat "Jip", commented Danny. "It must be wonderful to have such a uncomplicated life".

His mother was making bread as he entered the kitchen. She dusted the flour off her hands "Your father will not be best pleased you spending so much time seeing the Yankee away and now the rain has arrived". Danny was tempted to say, "Ma I don't give a hoot what da does or says".

"She didn't ask you to run away with her", teased Tess.

Danny decided to find out what his mother thought about the age difference. "Ach no", answered Danny. "Ten years is too big an age gap for a serious relationship to develop".

"What do you mean, what about me and your da, that was a much wider age gap". "Aye", said Danny. "But it would have been the opposite way around with me and Emma. I, the man was the younger"

As she put the dough into the baking tin, she replied. "Maybe or maybe not, you both seemed to hit it off together".

"I suppose we did", answered Danny. "She was a lovely lassie, she said she'd be delighted if I visited her sometime. He could feel the tears welling up inside again so he made the excuse "I better be away down to the bog".

His mother had detected his sadness somehow, as he headed towards the door he was stopped by her gentle call "Danny" she wiped her hands on her apron "I know how you feel". She threw her arms around him and give him a hug. He could feel the warm tears trickle down his cheek.

"Thanks ma", he blurted out. Then he was gone.

She didn't go back right away to her baking but went up the yard to the back gate. "At least we were lucky granny was in bed" she thought "she wouldn't know what to make of it all".

She leaned on the gate and looked away down the valley. Her thoughts stared back to that night when she saw Leo for the last time. She was eighteen the same age as Danny and the only thing that kept her from going insane was the solid promise that he would write to her. The months and months of waiting and the slow realization that nothing was going to materialise, all this handling between Emma and Danny had brought it flooding back. She could see the bright change in attitude in Danny just like herself when she first met Leo. She sincerely hoped Danny wouldn't get hurt as much as she did.

CHAPTER 12

For the next week or so Danny couldn't find the energy to re-join his pre Emma life. Every second day or so he cycled down to Pats house and had a look around. He pretended he was concerned for the safety of the house and contents but he was really hoping that by some stroke of luck he'd find Emma there. He walked all the places they used to walk watched the rabbits eating away unconcerned in the hallow of the back field. Soon this would end too. The land was now up for letting and as soon as the tenant moved his stock in he'd have to curtail his visits to the house only.

One evening when he came back from his walk he found Midge Pats old collie dog scratching at the front door. The evening Cathal Green had found Pat slumped on the bales of hay dead, at his feet he found Midge lying contently asleep. He brought him home as he thought it best, for he wasn't sure how long it was since he had eaten. Danny decided to bring him the half mile down to Greens again but as he made his way down the lane he met Cathals wife coming looking for Midge.

"When we let him out", said Mrs Green. "He always makes for here and spends his time searching the byres and sheds for Pat". "Fortunately he follows me back down to our house. I suppose he knows that's where he gets fed".

As Mrs Green and the dog headed down the lane and with Midge looking around mournfully now and again another sadness was felt by Danny. All the little items that made up Pats life was gone. His dog, his livestock all his farm implements and tools and he thought is this the way it ends for everybody. He then made up his mind it would be vital to marry and have off spring.

After a week or so he and Bosco was meeting again in the mornings at the crossroads. Bosco kept prodding looking for more information of his liaison with Emma but Danny never said much. The silence seemed to shroud the whole affair with mystique. He resumed his relationship with Alice. At first her attitude was frosty and indeed Danny didn't really care. He had an idea this affair wasn't long lasting. Bosco's relationship with Susan had grown. In fact it often bored Danny listening to Bosco singing her praises. "I think we are going out with those two too long", remarked Danny. "If we pulled back a bit and let the whole things cool down it might help us in the long run".

"What do you mean let the whole thing cool down", asked Bosco. "You'd think by you they were a tractors that was overheating".

Danny let the conversation peter out. Anything for a quiet life but he was already planning on ways of gathering enough money for the airfare to America. As he lay in bed at night he could visualise himself at a busy airport and seeing Emma waving over to him. He would know all the answers in a short time to all the questions he had in his head. He resumed football training. It was June now and games were coming thick and fast. He was playing very well. He had established himself as one of the team's midfielders. He was surprised how much stronger he'd become from last year.

He heard two old supporters talking one day when they didn't know he was listening "Young Higgins is going to be a good one", one said to the other. "Another year and he could turn out to be county material".

"Aye" remarked the other "that big gulpin who plays for St Pats at midfield won't push him about much longer". At least for now they were topping the league. He decided to spend some of his earnings on a small transistor radio he'd spied in Cassie Byrnes catalogue. The size of the transistor radio, which was now on the market delighted him. It wasn't much bigger that a cigarette box and ran on a tiny battery, not like what he'd been used to at home.

He told Bosco his intentions and invited him to accompany him to Cassie house to place the order.

"No no", Bosco protested. "I can't let that woman see me cause I am behind in the payments on the bracelet I bought for Susan's birthday. I asked the auld fella for a couple more bob and he let a ring of curses out of him that wasn't ordinary, says he "I'll sell the damned farm and give you the whole lot" so that was that"

"I'll tell you what I'll do", Danny replied. "I picked up a few bob for helping Emma with a few things at her Uncle Pats and I'm going to pay fully for my radio and I'll bring your payments up to date as well"

"I couldn't possibility ask you to do that", answered Bosco.

Danny cut in, "why not"? I have the money and I know if it was the other way around you wouldn't see me stuck".

Bosco reluctantly agreed, so they made their way down. Danny placed the order for the radio and Bosco paid up his debt.

"Thanks", said Bosco. "I hope it won't be too long until I'm able to pay you back. This courting is a costly business. Susan suggested the other night we should go to the seaside for a few days in August. She says she'll be able to subscribe because she's just got an evening job in Milligan's Shop".

"Well there you are", Danny replied. "Your sorted". I hope Alice isn't of the same notion, for I can assure you it won't be happening".

"Ach! Why not, look at the craic we'd have and maybe things might heat up a bit. You know more intimate".

"I wouldn't be so sure", answered Danny. Damn it she was a right wee court until the mission was here three months ago. Whatever those missioners told the woman she became real frosty after".

"They would have spouted out the same thrash they told us men, only turned it around" suggested Bosco "Remember (mimicking the missioner) young men be wary of sly girls who knowingly use heavy petting to bring innocent lads to a state of arousal and then the young men would force themselves on them and then the girls would cry rape. If you find yourself in such a situation be it in her home, in the cinema or in a car I'm warning you to leave, if not you'll be committing a mortal sin. If you don't confess it in confession you'll burn forever in the depths of hell".

"Do you know Bosco you missed your vocation you should have been a missioner",

"Remember we were sitting beside Marys Jimmy, that big goofy looking creative from the other side of the parish" said Bosco and his face become redder and redder the more your man preached".

"That's right", answered Danny, and I whispered if he gave anymore details your man's face would burst. Well after the mission there was a sharp decline in passion on Alice's part: No Sir, I'll not be spending money on bringing Miss McAree to the seaside".

"I will also have to disappoint Susan. August is a busy time on the farm and then there's that frequent problem of cash" I could see me explaining to Papa McNamee why I wouldn't be available to lend a hand in the meadow and then asking him for a large amount of money I could find myself racing down the road with a pitchfork protruding from my backside and him in hot persuit".

Ten days has now passed since Emma left. Danny made it his business to meet the postman most mornings in hope that had have a letter from her. "She has time now to get settled back in at home", he thought. He had decided to make plans to travel over to the U.S sometime in the spring. Most nights he would fall asleep thinking about her and how he could finance this trip. He even thought if he hinted to her how difficult he was finding to raise the air fare she might send some money over. After all if she was keen to see him why wouldn't she. Three weeks from the day she left a letter arrived. Unfortunately he hadn't met the postman that day so it was waiting for him in the house. His mother had gone to the village so when he asked had the postman any mail it was left up to his granny to tell him that indeed a very important looking letter had arrived for him. She made it plain that she was anxious to know who was the sender. She set herself to hear all the contents but when Danny stuck it in his pocket and left she wasn't best pleased. He went into the back of the turf shed where he knew no one would see and sat down on a bag of turf. His heart was pounding as he read the address. Then he took out his penknife and coushiously opened the envelope. He could find a faint smell of perfume, two photographs fell out, he read,

Dear Danny,

I hope this finds you well. I'm at last settled back to my boring old life again, the work accumulated when I was away and now its nose to the grindstone, shoulder to the wheel to catch up but I'll get there. I must thank you again firstly for all your help before and during the auction but mainly for the best three weeks I've had in my life. The weather was kind to us, my father assured me it is seldom, you have three weeks of unbroken good weather in Ireland. I know I left pretty abrubtly that last day but honestly I was afraid if I lingered too long I'd have sent the taxi man away and told him I was staying another while. I got the photos developed we took and I've sent you two of the best, one of each of us. I showed yours to my sister "My god she said what a handsome hunk of an Irishman" "cool it I warned her, hands off, he's all mine". I'll close now, don't forget that invitation still stands and if you were coming give me a few week notice I could take time off and show you the sights of upstate New York. Yes we have fine scenery here aswell (but not as quaint as around your place). Drop me a line. I've been looking forward to hearing from you, your loving friend, Emma XXXX

Danny folded it over and examined the two photographs "Jesus he thought even in Pats wellingtons and jacket she still looked stunning. He unfolded the letter and was reading it again when he heard his mother calling him. He put all back in the envelope and went to see what his mother wanted him for. Later on in the evening his granny again hinted about the letter, she had noticed it was an airmail stamp and done everything in her power to find out more, "Granny" said Tess "that's was addressed to Danny so it's none of our business what's in it, personally I think the government in America wants him to be the next president" That night after Granny had gone to bed and Dan was out on his Ceilie, Danny showed the two photos to his mother "My goodness she's a fine looking girl" commented Tess "I can see a fair share of her father in her, he wasn't half handsome as well". In the days that followed he took the letter out and read it trying to construct appropriate reply in his mind. He showed the photograph of Emma to Bosco pointing out that she was wearing her uncles wellies and jacket "Ah! Now she's a real humdinger no doubt" claimed Bosco if the circumstances were right I think no matter what the big missioner said you'd commit sin with her and take your chances of not going to hell". About a week or so after her letter came he sat down one night in his bedroom and wrote her a reply. He said, definitely he was now making plans to visit the U.S the following year, he did mention that the money of the fare would be the deciding factor what time of the year it would be. The quicker he could gather it up, the sooner he could go. He thought that should give her a good opening of saying she would lend him some. It would also give him an indication how serious she was about their relationship. "A speedy reply is what's needed", he thought.

CHAPTER 13

As the days lengthened Danny and Bosco as well as their rendezvous in the morning at the crossroads they'd often meet in the evenings. The evenings when they met Alice and Susan changed to Fridays when they would go to the cinema or out the road for a walk. The weather usually decided which. Danny went to football training on Tuesdays and a match was played most Sundays.

One evening Danny decided his radio must surely have arrived with Cassie so he called for Bosco and they travelled down to her house. His purchase was there and as he had already paid for it, four pounds, nothing more was owing.

"I'll have to come up with another few bob in a fortnights time and pay another instalment", announced Bosco. "I told my mother last week how much I really liked Susan and might need a few shillings more each week to take her places. She was very understanding, a lot more than I could say about the aul fella. "She gave me a ten shilling note, not bad eh".

The radio was a great success. They spent the next few evenings tuning into different stations, both Alice and Susan was very impressed and both suggested it would make a fine Christmas box.

That night as they cycled home Bosco let out a curse "Look what you and your danged radio has done now, put notions in those girls heads".

"I don't think it'll affect me", replied Danny. "I don't intend to be courting Alice at Christmas".

The first evening Danny brought the radio home, there was mixed reactions "That's a grand yoke", said Tess. "It'll save the batteries of this one in here. As well you can bring it to the bog and all the neighbours can hear the midday news from it".

Granny's response was different, she wanted to know where he'd got it and the cost. Danny knew from a conversation a few nights earlier between her and Edmund Coyle that none of the two of them favoured items being bought on easy payment so for devilment he said that he had sent away for it out of Cassie Byrnes catalogue and he'd agreed to pay four shillings a month.

Granny shifted herself on the chair "That danged being will wreck the country, her and catalogue. Easy payments be damned you'll see how easy they'll be. Didn't you hear Edmund Coyle say the other night he knew a woman who bought a tilley lamp that way and she happened to become sick and missed one payment, this bloke arrived one morning took the tilley lamp with him. He says that catalogue is the worst thing that came into the country.

"Ach it's not all bad", Tess replied. "It'll keep him in gossip as he goes around the country scandalising people.

As Danny made to leave he turned the radio up loud "You must admit granny she's a whole good one".

Later that evening at the crossroads he related the story to Bosco. As he kicked a stone down the road Bosco announced "That's a begrudging ould devil, that boy. I hope nobody tells him I've made a purchase by easy payments, he'll make me the laughing stock of the country.

"I wouldn't be too bothered about him", said Danny. "Some night when he's in our house I must announce that I'm behind in the payments already and wonder would there be any chance of him giving me a loan. He'll have it over the whole country in no time".

One evening at the crossroads Bosco was already there and as Danny approached Bosco announced "I got another letter from Martin Carlin today: "Do you know he's getting worse with all his bumming".

"What is he at now, asked Danny, probably running some big airline".

"No but he's running a large section of McAlpines, the largest contractor in England", said Bosco. "He's in charge of fifteen sites and all he does, every day is drive in a new Mercedes car from one site to the next, making sure the foremen have no problems, he says his big concern is not having enough tradesmen or labourers. He says he'll be home in September and his father and Owenie, his brother are going back with him".

"How could any of those two leave here" remarked Danny. "Owenie never leaves Conway's corner in the village. If he left it I've a notion it would fall. The father with his sore back is never out of the doctors surgery. If he left Doctor Casey would have his workload cut in half".

"He was asking would me and yourself not be interested in going back with him" said Bosco.

"He's a mystery to me", said Danny. How well he's done since he's left. Before he went he was completely useless and that was at everything. I remember he played football for a while but every night at training he was sure to get hurt and had to quit. He started work with McKenna the building contractor. How long did it last, a day and a half. He said his heart was racing too hard and if he didn't go home and lie down he was afraid it would come out through his chest".

"He was also saying he and another bloke, he calls every man a bloke, owns a famous race horse between them and the next time its running he'll drop me a line to tell me so I can put a few bob on it" said Bosco.

Danny let a giggle "A decent bloody man no doubt". "What about his girlfriends, any big news on that front"?

"Oh! aye he met this girl at some show jumping event and they went out for a while", said Bosco. "She is a niece or a cousin or something to Prince Philip but he had to break it off in case they'd find out he came from a big republican family

"Republican family my foot said Danny, he probably thinks he some kind of bloke such as Che Chuvara. No organisation would have him, not even the Legion of Mary.

"I told him in my letter to him", said Bosco. "That you were hoping to get on the county team this year. He asked was it the county council you were hoping to get on".

"He's a quare sarcastic hoor so he is", remarked Danny.

"The odd thing about him is after all he supposed to have, his address is still at Mrs Murrays which I presume is a lodging house" said Bosco. "Oh! and when he'd finished he put at the foot of it, p.s the my mother told me Pat Burke was dead, I told her if the wee farm came up for sale be sure and let him know, he'd make sure he would buy it.

Danny pulled out the transistor radio from his pocket "I bet he hasn't a yoke like this" he said tuning it into a station.

CHAPTER 14

Weeks went past and Danny was becoming anxious Emma hadn't replied as quickly as he'd have liked. He met the postman most days but nothing was forthcoming. Every now and then Tess would ask him if he'd any late word. When he told her none she always stressed not to expect too much. His father never said anything about Emma, Leo or the whole event which had taken place. If he realised something was different about Danny since Pats wake he never mentioned it.

One evening he met Johnny the Spade coming home from wherever he was working. Danny had the radio in his pocket before Johnny arrived his length he switch it off. After a few minutes of asking Johnny how well his new spade, the one Emma gave him, was doing and Johnny was in the midst of telling Danny he still hadn't used it, he switched on the radio.

Johnny gulped with surprise "What's that you've there Danny"?

"I don't know", said Danny, "that noise has been coming out of my stomach all day I'm going to see the doctor about it tomorrow"

Johney threw back his head and let a hearty laugh, "Stop your codding Danny it's a wireless of some kind".

Danny produced the radio "What do you think of that yoke Johney", asked Danny. "You should have one fitted to your spade. Imagine listening to your favourite programmes all day long".

Johney took the radio and examined it "boys oh boys", said Johney, such a dainty wee thing but where's the batteries". "This is a new type of radio Johney", explained Danny. "It's called a transistor and the battery is that small it fits inside it".

"What will they think of next", Johney replied. "But then of course this television is a great affair. Noel Delaney who owns the pub in the town got me to make a few drains in the garden out the back, he has a television I watched it for a while when I was taking me evening's tea".

"I heard he couldn't get you out of the place", fibbed Danny. "Ah your only codding Danny I didn't stay that long", laughed Johney. "You're a terrible boyo Danny for taking a hand with a body". My Mother Lord rest her was a great one for the wireless, she used to dance with the sweeping brush around the floor. Every now and then she would let a whoop out of her, then when my father came home from work she'd grab him and both of them would swing round the floor, they seemed so happy".

"How many was in your family Johnny"? asked Danny.

"There was eight of us, four boys and four girls. Aye they seemed so healthy and happy but we were all still young when they both died, within a year of each other, mammy first then daddy. I was the oldest, just eleven sure I couldn't provide for them all so the authories split us up. The youngest four went and stayed with two aunts. Myself and the other three was put into an orphanage. I hated it that much I ran away several times, when I was fourteen I started to work for a farmer. He wasn't a very nice man, he took advantage of me and since so did many others. I moved up from Donegal to these parts with another fella and mostly we were threated with kindness. We worked hard, slept in barns or anywhere we could find. Joe the other fella went over to Scotland to gather potatoes but I stayed here, working a day here and a day there. Many nights I'd cry myself to sleep when I'd remember mummy and daddy dancing to the music coming from the radio. Life can be cruel Danny, very cruel".

"What about your brothers and sisters, where did they end up?" enquired Danny.

"My brother Frank and my Sister Kitty both died young but the rest eventually ended up in a America with another aunt and has done well for themselves. I don't hear that much from them. I must be going I'll say it again that's a great contraption Danny".

The days went by and accumulated into weeks no letter arrived from Emma. Every day Danny became more disheartened. He was now questioning if he'd read the situation wrong, maybe Emma didn't really mean anything when she gave him those passionate hugs and kisses. Maybe that's what Americans do. Still when he'd look at her photo he hoped sincerely more might develop from their relationship. With no correspondence arriving, the busy days on the farm, football playing in full swing and the friendship between him and Alice still on going, time slipped past quickly. Every so often he called down to Pats house and checked it over to make sure there was no intruders. He was coming from it one evening when he met Johney the spade coming.

Almost right away he realised that there was something not right with Johney.

"What's the matter Johney"? Danny asked. "What's bothering you"?

"Do you know what they're saying", said Johney. "They're saying I stole Pat Burkes spade. What do you think of that Danny".

"Just hold on a minute Johney who's accusing you of stealing Pats spade", questioned Danny.

"I don't his right name but he's known as Liam the Rook, I was back yesterday again with your man who owns the pub in the village and he and two other men were in drinking and said I was a disgrace stealing a dead man's spade".

"Don't listen to them pack of hounds, they're only trying to upset you. I'll go and tell them I was there when Emma gave you the spade, but they've already harmed my good name", answered Johney. "Everybody who came into the bar all day yesterday they brought out to where I was digging in the back garden and said "This is the thief who stole Pat Burke's new spade".

Danny realised that Johney was deeply annoyed and it was going to take a lot of convincing that these boyos were really trying to rise Johney's temper. Liam Ruddy or Liam the Rook which he was better known as was a hateful gulpin. He was always trying to rag somebody. He didn't have a steady job but with his pals he'd cut and sell firewood. The proceeds was always spent right away on alcohol. More often than not he'd pick at someone until a row would develop. Everybody was wary of them and would stay well away from their company.

"You know me Danny", said Johney. "I never stole anything in my life, nothing. If somebody gave something to me fair enough but I wouldn't steal anything, not even an egg".

"Look Johney I'm going into the town tomorrow and I'll tell your man in the pub what these boys are saying and to tell them not to be spreading lies", said Danny.

"Oh, don't do that Danny", insisted Johney "For they are vicious. The Rook pulled out a knife yesterday and he held it up to my face saying your throat should be cut for doing such a dirty act, he's dangerous Danny, a madman".

"But still", Danny replied, "we can't let the hound off." Danny could see what he was saying was not calming Johney down anything. Danny tried again "Look Johney stay away from the town for a wee while, you are not the first those boys have riled, they're at it all the time, spreading rumours, picking fights, always in some kind of trouble. Promise me you will calm down, I know and the whole country knows you wouldn't take a thing that's not your own".

"I hope so Danny", said Johney. "If the people in the country believed them I wouldn't get any more work.

"That'll not happen Johney you'll see", announced Danny, "go home and don't worry about it and I'll see the bar owner tomorrow."

As Johney trudged down the road Danny looked over his shoulder at him. "That's still not a happy man" he thought to himself. The next day Danny and his father came back to the house from the hay field for their dinner.

"There's a letter for you" his mother announced "It's those yankees again hoping it won't be long before you go over to rule the country" granny said jokingly again. They all waited in anticipation for him to open the letter and even though he wanted to he put it in his pocket without saying a word. After dinner he causally left for his room. His heart was pounding and his hands shaking so much he made several attempts to open it. It was now nine weeks since he had answered her last letter. Again a photograph fell out of it. It was one of Emma and some fella. He opened up and read.

Dear Danny,

Delighted to hear from you again and glad to hear you and all your family are fine. Find enclosed a photograph of Toni and myself, Toni has been a boyfriend of mine for some years now, not all the time for his work took him around the world. At last he secured a post in the U.S and we decided to celebrate by becoming engaged to be married last month. If your still interested in travelling here, I'd be only too glad to show you around or maybe you'd wait until the year after next, you could come over for our wedding.

Danny read the finish of the letter but wasn't taking anything in, he felt a terrible surge of sadness filling his head. All the dreams, hopes and aspirations gone down the Swanee.

"It was always too good to be true", he thought. It was just a romantic idea with too many differences to overcome to make it reality. Age and cultural gaps. Also, how far apart they were from each other. When it was thought over it really was never on, still for a few months the feeling was magic and now it's like a death which somehow must be got over. He heard his father shout to him not to be too long. He looked at the photo blanking out Toni "Christ" he whispered to himself "she looks more fabulous there than before".

He folded up the letter and hid it in the drawer where her other one was and went down to the kitchen. Again granny shuffled on her chair waiting for some announcement that wasn't forthcoming, his mother waited until he went outside and followed him up the yard. "How's Emma"? she enquired. "Fine, just fine", answered Danny. "She just got engaged to some Italian buff" "Ah Danny, I'm sorry", said Tess. "I had a fair idea you thought something might come of it but maybe it's all for the best".

"Probably", Danny replied, "but it doesn't feel that way just now". He could feel his tears welling up inside, his mother come towards him and gave him a hug.

"I know how you feel and I know you'll get over it", she said.

As he worked at the hay he picked through the whole affair looking for positives. It was himself he reckoned was to blame. If he'd opened his eyes he'd saw it was never serious, just a fleeting thing.

"I feel so rotten", he thought. "I wish I'd wake up and find it was all a dream".

CHAPTER 15

That evening he decided to keep his promise to Johney and talk to Noel Delaney of the Crescent bar to make sure Liam the Rook didn't annoy Johney any further about stealing the spade because it had annoyed him so much. He parked his bike and went into the bar. He wasn't sure what kind of a reception he would get.

"Hello Noel". said Danny "I was talking to Johney the spade last night and he was very annoyed because the Rook accused him of stealing Pat Burke's spade but I know he didn't for I was there when Emma, Pat's niece gave the spade to him".

"Ach! Sure I think the Rook was only codding" said Noel.

"Your probably right" Danny replied, "but you know poor Johney is a bit innocent and took it all in earnest, maybe you could have a word with the Rook to lay off Johney".

"All right I will try" answered Noel, "but the Rook is an ignorant creature it might make him go stronger at Johney". Just then the door opened and in steps Liam the Rook "Here" continued Noel, "you can tell him yourself now".

"Tell me what?" asked the Rook.

"This fella here thinks your being too sore on Johney about stealing Pat Burke's spade" said Noel.

"I was only telling the truth sonny boy", said the Rook. "What other way did he get it. He was seen with it one evening before the auction".

"Yes and the reason he had it was because Pats niece Emma gave it to him", answered Danny. "Actually I saw Johney come along the road and Emma had just told me if I wanted any of Pat's tools I could have them, I said there's a man who would be delighted to have the new spade so I called to him and he came up and Emma gave him the spade, he was over the moon. She gave me Pats bike aswell".

The Rook started to snigger "We've only your word about that, there's a good chance both of you stole the spade and the bike".

Danny could find his temper rising he'd heard many reports of the Rook, how vicious he could be but Danny was in a foul mood after his bad luck that morning. "I'll make it clear again, nobody stole anything, we were both given these items by Emma".

"There's rumours going about said the Rook "that you were sagging that one. I saw her myself cycling out every evening to Pat's, those Americans can't get enough of it. Well? Were you shagging her"?

"That's for you to find out", Danny replied, "but I'm warning you stop torturing poor Johney".

Danny went to leave but the Rook caught him by the arm swung him round shouting "Warning me". He went to throw a punch at Danny but Danny ducked, and then landed a uppercut straight on the Rooks chin, tossing him between two chairs and landing him under a table.

"Stop it", roared Noel, "if you want to fight, do it outside".

Danny went over to where the Rook was laying "Come on if you want more, there's plenty where that came from you no good lousy tosser, come on, I'll be waiting".

As he left the Rook was still struggling to arise off the floor and Danny could hear him telling Noel he thought his jaw was broken Noel was replying "Served you right".

Danny rode home. "The news of me fighting in the bar in the town will probably be home before me" he thought. "Where were you"? his mother asked, "I just cycled into the town to see if the match is still on on Sunday" lied Danny.

Next morning at the crossroads he told Bosco about the whole incident. "Jayus, you broke the Rooks jaw" exclaimed Bosco "there'll be trouble about that. He'll not let this lie, probably he'll be looking for damages. Quare awkward customer".

"Aye, I know that Bosco" replied Danny, but he swung first and only I saw his fist coming it would have been me who'd got injured. Anyway Noel Delaney was witness and Johney will confirm that the Rook was harassing him".

"Well, make sure and watch your back", said Bosco. "I wouldn't trust thon boy, he could hit you with a stick or something from behind".

Danny kicked a stone down the road " Yesterday wasn't a good day for me overall, I got a letter from Emma saying she got engaged last month and will be married the year after next to some Italian buck" I thought myself it was only friendship", explained Danny, that was until the last day. The signals she gave me that day made me believe it could be more serious. I just happened to read the whole danged situation all wrong".

"I better be going", said Bosco. "I might happen to be in town later on, my mother wants a parcel posted, I'll make enquires if anybody knows much about the dust up". "Ach, they'll know it all", answered Danny, and it'll be his version. As well you'll find it'll be blown out of all proportion".

As Bosco headed down the road he shouted back "I'll see you here this evening at half eight".

That evening Bosco was waiting as Danny arrived at the crossroads "You were bloody right" announced Bosco. "The whole place was full of it, I didn't even make it into the town before I heard a version of it from the chief gossiper himself Edmund Coyle."

"Ah jayus", said Danny, "not that blast he'll thrive on telling it around the whole country including up at home. I thought I might be able to keep it from them. What was he saying"?

"He was trudging up Flanagans bray so I stopped with him. I had no sooner took me foot off the pedal until he was off, Mrs Cadden had told him of this big row in the Cresent Bar. She had told him as far as she could make out they were both drunk and that you came out with your fists closed and shouting. Then a minute later the Rook appeared being armed by Noel Delaney who drove away with him in the car and the blood pumping from him. He had talked to others but nobody could shed any light on what the reasons was for it, only that both parties seemed drunk. The postmistress Mena Slattery was telling a man who was in just before me it was probably girl related. She said it wouldn't end there because the Ruddys would be looking for compensation. As I was leaving the village who did I meet only Father McElrone. He stopped and quizzed me but I pretended I knew nothing. As he walked away shaking his head saying "Thugs the lot of them"

"He didn't say that", queried Danny. Bosco laughed "No I made the thugs bit up but he did say there was a lot of violence going on and he'd have to preach a sermon on it".

They debated the subject for some while, wondering how Alice would take it. A younger brother of the Rooks played football on the senior team, how would he take it. When Danny wondered how the three at home would deal with it Bosco announced he knew exactly how his father would deal with it, if it was him. He'd have a fairly good try at beating the living daylights out of him or the Rook or both of them.

Dusk has fallen before they parted. As he walked home Danny decided he'd tell his mother and father what exactly happened and he hoped the whole affair could be kept from the granny. As soon as he opened the door and saw Edmund Coyle sitting in the corner he knew they had already been informed. The house fell into a uneasy silence. Danny tried to act normally and nothing was said for a minute.

Granny brushed her cardigan with her hand and Danny had realised some time ago it was a signal she had something to get off her chest. "Edmund was just telling us about the carry on you where at in the village yesterday".

Danny had a drink of water, "Ach that, sure it was nothing", he said.

"You'll find out it'll be more than nothing when you're finished with that Ruddy latchaco", granny replied.

"What the devil was it all about"? queried his father. "It was nothing really", Danny explained. "He made a swing at me, I ducked and I hit him instead".

"You broke his jaw", granny replied, "or what in the name of heavens were you doing in a pub in the early evening"?

"Look" his mother butted in, if Danny doesn't want to tell us that's alright. I know there's already lies being told. Somebody told Edmund that you were drunk but when you arrived home here at half past nine you were totally sober". Danny let a nervous laugh "Of course I was sober because I still have my pledge, I don't drink".

His father had a fair idea they'd had been fed only rumours from Edmund and it would be a benefit if Danny would relate his side of the story. "Damn it you still haven't told us why you got involved with him" said Dan.

"Right said Danny, this is exactly how it happened, the evening before last I happen to meet Johney the spade on the road and the poor man was demented. He had been making a few drains in a garden at the back of the Cresent bar for Noel Delaney. The Rook came out and called Johney a thief. He said he'd stolen Pat Burkes new spade. No matter how Johney tried to explain how he came to have the spade the Rook kept on and on telling him he was a liar as well as a thief. I tried my best to calm him down and I promised I'd have a wee talk with Noel and tell him to keep the Rook away from Johney, so I went to Noel yesterday evening unfortunately as I was leaving who came in to the bar only the Rook, so I asked him politely to leave poor Johney alone as he was a bit simple. Of course he said he wasn't that simple when he was able to steal the spade, then he closed his fist and swung at me but I saw it coming so I ducked and then I got him square on the chin. Then I walked out and came home"

Danny waited for a reaction. His mother was the first to speak. "Good for you son, a hound like the Rook torturing poor Johney, you done the right thing"

Danny looked over at his father a smirk covered his face as if to say "I'm proud of you". Edmund made no comment.

After a little while Granny queried. "How did Johney have Pats spade if he didn't steal it"?

Danny could fell his temper beginning to rise, as he explained "Emma gave it to him, one evening we were standing in Pats yard putting things in place for the auction and she asked me if I wanted to take the new spade home with me and just then I saw Johney coming down the road, I shouted down to him to come up. Emma presented him with the spade, he said he'd pay her for it but she wasn't having any of it. Let me tell you he went away a very proud man. That's how he came to have Pats spade.

Granny once again was brushing her cardigan. "It's just Edmund had heard from several people he was seen up at Pats mooching about a couple of days before the auction".

Danny saw red, all the frustration of the last few days had built up into an anger he had never witnessed before. He got up from where he was sitting, shouted towards Edmund, "I suppose you also heard I stole Pats bike. Well let me tell you I stole no bike, Johney stole no spade but its big mouths like you going round the country spreading lies and scandal that should be taken out and horsewhipped".

He turned round from where he was standing, lifted a mug off the table and fired it hitting the wall above Edmund's head smashing into smithereens with the pieces raining down on Edmund's head like confetti. He walked out banging the door as he went. The night was a beautiful calm moonlight night. Half way down the lane he turned into the field by the river. He felt wretched because even though his temper hadn't subsided he knew he'd let his parents down, with his outburst. He travelled down the hedge between two of their fields and sat down on a large flat stone where he often rested. Down below the river that acted as the march between their farm and McSwiggans was quite visible in the moonlight, every now and then the moon caught the ripples making them look as if they were dancing on top of the water. Suddenly he heard movement further up the hedge and within seconds Jip was at his side and snuggled up to him.

"Good aul pal", he said, "you're so lucky you haven't any serious worries" "There'll be a poor reception for a body when I return", he thought. The last few days had so many sets backs, things he just couldn't have imagined when he woke yesterday morning. Losing Emma was bad, the fight with the Rook wasn't really his fault but this outburst was surely the worst of all. He started to think what would be his best move for the future. Here he was going on nineteen, hasn't as much money buy a good suit, slaving away day in day out just surviving. His parents look after him well and he always has the basic needs, food, shoes, clothes. It's as much as they could afford but surely there must be something better out there something that would give him more satisfaction. That's why he'd put so much faith in his relationship with Emma. It would have broken this monotonous cycle. Of course he could still go to the US but it wouldn't be the same now. In her letter even though she said she would show him around it seemed more distant than before and she didn't mention any notion of forwarding a loan to help him to make the trip. In another month or so after the potatoes were dug there would be no reason why he couldn't go out to work with a contractor. He knew a few he could ask but with short days and the weather turning rougher it could be hard enough to obtain work.

"Ach to hell" he said to himself "We must look at the positives I'll wait to October and see then if there'd be any openings on the job front. What's that saying, it's better to light one candle then to sit and curse the dark". He rose from where he was sitting and sauntered down the field to the river edge, he thought to himself he must be determined to change his life around. There'll be opposition from the folks at home but it was his life and he should be allowed to live it as he wanted.

"Come on Jip" he said to the dog, "it's time to go home and face the music".

He had been out over an hour and hopefully they'd be in bed. If they started to rant and rave and give too much grief he just reply he was leaving and would seek employment in some other part of the country. He'd point out his side of the story and maybe they'd accept it.

As he gingerly opened the door he could see the only one up was his mother. She was patching a pair of trousers, she didn't look up or say anything. Danny poured himself a glass of milk and sat down, they sat in silence for a while.

"Sorry ma", said Danny, "for what happened earlier, "Yes" his mother replied, "that was some outburst or what the devil come over you Danny"?

"Bosco had told me earlier he was talking to Edmund coming home from the town", said Danny, so I knew for certain he would be here tonight to relay all to you three. It doesn't matter to that man where its truth or lies as long as its gossip, he'll spread it".

"Ach! I know son that's really all he has to live for", answered his mother. "Down through the years it was always the same with Edmund he always put his own spin on stories".

"As well he always running down the youth", said Danny. "As if he wasn't young himself one time or maybe he wasn't". His mother let a giggle "That could be debatable"

"I supposed da and granny is going to have me hung, drawn and quartered" commented Danny.

"Your da isn't too concerned", said Tess. I explained to him how you'd received disappointing news from Emma yesterday. That's the first time he knew you had some feelings for Emma. As for her ladyship, she announced in front of Edmund the priest would have to be brought out and give you a good talking to". Of course it was our fault, we had you spoiled, out galavanting every night to football, dances and the cursed picture house". "I have said this before ma and I'll say it again nothing stands still. What was the norm in your time wouldn't satisfy the young ones today", said Danny. "What kept the young ones happy in Granny's time wouldn't have done in your time and that is really the crux of the matter, not only that but the teenagers in thirty years time looking back will all agree, our generation was very easily pleased with our bicycles, tilley lamps and a film now and again".

"Here away to your bed now" instructed Tess "and I shouldn't be saying this, don't worry too much about flying off the handle at Edmund, there's any amount of folks through the country would clap you on the back for what you've done".

As he headed towards the door he turned rounding saying "Thanks ma that has made me feel better, sorry for boring you but I think things will change a lot in the next few years with electricity, cars, television and better houses. Well at least that's the future according to Danny Higgins".

The next morning there was no speech from his father, usually he would make some comment maybe about the weather or one of the animals, but this morning, nothing. As usual he brought the can of milk down to the road and sauntered up to the crossroads. A minute later Bosco appeared. Right away Danny told him of the handling the night before in the house.

Bosco threw back his head and laughed heartily "Jayus Higgins your turning into a wild man, do you know something it might curb that hoor from going around the country gossiping".

"How did the aul pair take it"? "I was only talking to my mother after I came back", replied Danny, she more or less said what your after saying but granny now she is going to take me in hand herself. First thing, she's contacting the bishop or even maybe the pope to get him out to talk to me, then she's putting a stop to football, dances and especially them blasted movies. She's organising a mission to be held here at the crossroads. Men must wrap themselves with juke bags and all girls must wear two pairs of reinforces underwear".

"Ha ha, it's going to be a fun time all right", indicated Bosco. "Here I must be going, we've a big day's corn cutting in front of us, see you to night. Its ladies night".

"I mightn't have a lady to see", said Danny. "I'm sure McArees no doubt will have heard about the unsavoury incidents caused by yours truly and the romantic affair may have been cut short. Not, let me tell you that it'll break my heart for I think it has run its course".

CHAPTER 16

The breakfast was consumed and conversation was non existant. Lucky enough granny decided to lie on for a while. Danny and his father headed out to the cornfield. His father a hundred yards in front, Danny decided he would have to break the ice and he reckoned the best way would be to apologise. It was just finding the right time. Danny and his father had a fairly good relationship. When out in the fields they discussed the news and goings on in the country. His father wasn't a great one for going to functions. A couple of nights in the week especially in the winter time he'd ceildhe in some of the neighbours houses. Edmund Coyles being one of them. Danny reckoned with his father dying young, Dan was just ten when his father died, he was influenced by his mother and kept under her thumb. Danny never heard his father talking about going to dances or socialising in anyway. How himself and his mother met, courted and married was a mystery to Danny. His mother would have been a fine looking girl in her day and many people assured Danny she was lively, fond of dancing and had quite a few boyfriends. It was only lately when Leo was over for Pats wake and funeral and what was told to him by Emma and his mother herself, he realised her friendship with Leo was the real deal and when, for whatever reason it didn't workout, she married Dan, someone she could depend on. He was thrifty, he wouldn't ever see her wanting and wouldn't let her down. They had worked over an hour at the corn, his father mowing with the scythe and Danny tying it into sheaves. Being a fairly warm day his father sat down to rest.

"This is my chance", said Danny to himself. He made over to where his father was sitting when he was still a fair bit away, he said "I'm sorry Da for what happened last night, I was completely in the wrong".

His father was chewing a straw and didn't speak for about twenty seconds, to Danny it felt like twenty hours. Then he cleared his throat and spit out. "These things happen", he said. "I'd rather it hadn't happened for a few reasons. It gives granny ammunition to fire at us all. We have already heard a large amount after you left last night and no doubt there'll be more to come. As well Edmund will take nothing off it as he spreads it around the country. I knew he can be an aul gossip sometimes but he has nothing else to bother him. A fairly well off bachelor who's nearest relatives are about Glasgow and never comes near him".

"But he seems to get a great kick out of spreading scandal and other peoples woes through the country", Danny replied. "As well as that he's always running down young people. Was he never young himself"?

His father gave a little giggle. "Well I suppose he was young but I'd have to say he never done anything that youth do, not that I should be speaking for I suppose I didn't do many of them either but maybe with my father dying when I was ten left me with a fair share of work to do".

Danny sat down beside him "What was your Da like"? questioned Danny.

"I never heard much about him only that he fell off his bicycle coming home from the town and died a few days later".

"Well", answered Dan, "that's just part of the story. He was fond of the drink spent a lot of time in the pub. Then coming home one dark night he'd no lights on his bike he hit the range wall of the bridge at Fagan's lane. He was lying unconscious for several hours. He was in hospital for four days but never regained consciousness. That left me and granny. Money wasn't plentiful, my father had drank any that was about and more. He left a mighty lot of bills behind. Quite a few people thought we'd have to sell the farm but with hard work especially from your granny we held on to it. I'd have to say in those years Edmund was a great help. He was a few years older than me, kept two horses and done all our field work. You know putting in and taking out the crops. That's the reason, no matter what he does or says Granny won't let anybody say a bad word against him".

Danny shifted uneasily on his seat "I didn't know there was any good in him at any stage".

"Yes", his father replied, "it just shows, you should never judge people. They might have been different in the past. That is why granny is death on drink as well, seeing what happened to her husband. So when she heard you were in the pub the other evening she thought you started to booze".

"She should know me better than that" said Danny, anyway where would I find the cash to buy drink".

"Maybe the shortage of money isn't a whole bad thing", remarked Dan.

Danny realised, after what his father had told him that his crime of insulting Edmund in front of granny was greater that he thought. After work he decided to make few courteous remarks to granny hoping she'd respond in a civil manner but to no avail, she completely ignored him. Danny and Bosco met up as usual and cycled into the town to see the two girls. Danny was apprehensive how Alice would take the affair with The Rook.

"What in heavens name were you at"? asked Alice, fighting in a pub, I never knew you drank".

"Who said I drank", questioned Danny.

"Liam told us, he's a first cousin of mine", said Alice, he said he was minding his own business when you come over and clattered him, he said you were definitely drunk and you caught him unawares".

"So that was his version", said Danny. "Now listen to mine, go then and ask Noel Delaney who's version is the right one". Danny went on to explain to Alice what happened that evening and why he was in the bar. He was there to ask Noel to not let The Rook tease Johney the Spade. He explained how the Rook made a swing at him first and missed and how he landed a punch to the Rook chin.

"I wasn't in the bar any longer that three or four minutes and I wasn't drinking and I'm surprised and disappointed at you Alice believing I drink alcohol".

"Well I was only going by what Liam told us the other night", Alice replied.

It made Danny very cross, "Good enough then", said Danny, "it's up to yourself to believe me or The Rook".

"Don't call him that horrible name", Alice demanded "some people don't like him but"……

"I'll call him what I like", answered Danny, "and I'll tell you what, I'm away home, Ive something better to do than listen to people lying about me".

He turned and walked up the street to where his bike was parked and headed home leaving the three staring after him. "Another bloody row", he thought "when am I going to get my life sorted". As he cycled home as well a feeling anger he also felt a great sadness. By standing up for Johney he'd landed himself in one handling after another and disappointing quite a few along the way. Maybe it would be best if he could leave for a while. The trip to America was now a closed book. Where would he be going. Anyway where would he find the sort of money it would take. Another idea came into his head. What would be wrong with going back with Martin Carlin when he'd be home in a month's time. He still had most of the money Emma gave him, he could sell Pat Burke's bicycle and now with not having a girlfriend he should be able to save enough to pay his way over. The more he thought of this plan the more attractive it seemed. Maybe he could convince Bosco to go aswell. The crops would be mostly saved and they could return in the springtime in time to plant the crops for next year. His thoughts had lightened his mood. Now there was still a lot of convincing to do. He would have to start on Bosco. He wasn't sure how that would go. Then he had his parents to win over to the idea. It wouldn't be simple but he'd try his best.

"What a handling we had with Alice after you left", said Bosco. "Couldn't get her settled at all then when I said there had been a lot of lies told about you I was accused of taking sides. Susan then started to cry. There I was with two women blaring their heads off. Eventually we left Alice home, went to the chippie and things settled down. I promised Alice I'd try my best to bring you back".

"Well you shouldn't have bothered", answered Danny. "For I'm not going back".

There was a long silence before Bosco spoke. "I suppose your probably right you said a few things lately that you felt the affair with Alice was near at an end but I wouldn't like to stop taking Susan out. We got on well with each other and I think she would as well hope it would turn out long term".

"Well good luck to you both", said Danny. "Ive had a lot on my mind lately, I need to take a step back and settle my head. Why don't you tell Alice my parents don't want me to go near the town until all the hullabaloo about the incident with The Rook has settled down. Tell her as far as your concerned I'm still interested and will be back in a few weeks. In the meantime I'll stay away from the town for a while.

"This causes a problem for me", explained Bosco, for if we go to the pictures or anywhere I'd be expected to pay both of them in and that a large burden on my purse".

"Well then you may try and knock up another boyfriend for her" said Danny.

"Jaysus to hear you", Bosco replied. "You'd think a body could make a boyfriend out of a couple of bits of a four by two timber".

"I'll leave it with you", said Danny. "I might see you about this evening".

"Aye probably", answered Bosco. "Susan was wanting me to bring her to the circus, it's in the town this evening but I said I was too busy at home. You see I have to supply Cassie Byrne with another payment. I never seen anything that's comes around as quickly".

Danny had decided not to mention anything to Bosco about going back with Martin Carlin, he'd have too long to think about it. It would be much better coaxing him a few days before Martin left. A few days passed before Danny and Bosco met at the crossroads, "Hi! do you know what them two scoundrels done"? said Bosco. "They went to the circus and was seen leaving with Owenie Carlin and Henry Kerr walking hand and hand the feckers". Auld slippery Owenie was with Susan and the other boyo was linked with Alice. Was that sending out a statement or what"?

"Hoho! boy you may get out your six guns out and ride into town", suggested Danny. "I don't know much about the Kerr boy but Owenie Carlin thinks of himself as a bit of a Casanova. When were you to see Susan again"?

"With all the whinging and crying. I said I'd see her at the weekend. It's working out all right for you but I wouldn't like to lose Susan and especially not to Owenie bloody Carlin".

A prolonged discussion took place on the best way to approach Bosco's dilemma. It was agreed he'd need to contact her the following night and find out how serious this latest blip was. As the two boys went their separate ways Danny started to sing "On top of old smokey all covered with snow I lost my true love by courting to slow. From well down the road he could hear Bosco shouting "Would you shut your mouth". When Bosco contacted Susan again and put it to her she had been seen coming from the circus with

Owenie Carlin she admitted they walked up the town with the two boys but nothing else happened.

"Well at least nothing between Owenie and myself", she added, she wasn't sure about Alice and Henry Kerr but then with the row the week before, Alice classed herself now a free agent

"So everything is fine between you and Susan again", asked Danny. "You believe her".

"Aye I do", said Bosco. "I do think we were made for each other. Althought it'll be strange going to the pictures in the winter time without you".

"You and Henry will probably hit it off alright", said Danny. "The Kerr's are nice people and have a bit of wealth as well".

"I know but Susan was wondering how we could get you and Alice back together again" answered Bosco.

"We'll see", said Danny. "I'll not promise anything and it won't happen until the nights become longer".

A couple of weeks past and nothing exciting was happening Danny didn't appear near the town at night. He attended carnival dances a few nights in a different parish. When playing football no one bothered him or said anything about the row with The Rook, not even the Rook's brother who played on the team. Danny was playing very well and indeed was the star player a few times.

CHAPTER 17

Edmund Coyle started to ceilidh again. He was there one evening when Danny arrived home, both greeted each other civilly and Danny could sense relief on everyone in the house. Granny who had stayed frosty since the handling seemed to lighten up and indeed Danny felt better and hoped it was all cleared up.

Then one night near the end of August as Danny entered the house Edmund was in full flow "I tell you she's the width of the road. I never saw a vehicle like her. There's two big tail lights that lights up the whole place, when he brakes".

Danny's mother broke in "You haven't seen this great wagon Martin Carlin has home with him? Edmund met him on the road today and he's just been telling us about it".

"So he's home", Danny replied. "He is indeed", answered Edmund, he is looking like a millionaire. Dressed in a fine suit, shoes you could see yourself in, a fairly expensive looking wrist watch and not one ring but a number of them and then the vehicle. How in heavens name did he accumulate all that stuff the short time he's been away, eighteen months or so".

Granny let a dry cough "It'll be all on easy payments, that's the way they work over there, he'll be paying in for it until he's ancient. You'll find out the fancy taillights won't be as bright when he shoving out the last payment".

"Sush Granny", warned Tess, "you shouldn't say things like that. He's probably working long hours and earning good money".

"Working long hours", repeated Granny, when did any of his breed work long hours, no siree I know them down through the generations and dang the bit of them would work".

Edmund agreed, none of the older generation were too keen to work. "They always seemed to have something wrong with them", he added.

"But I'm sure you've seen it before", announced Tess, "of people who left this country with nothing and done well for themselves in England or America".

Danny couldn't wait until the next morning for he knew Martin would have called with Bosco.

"Oh! aye he called alright", said Bosco. "He drove up in this mighty yoke scattering hens and ducks everywhere. Was lucky our aul fella wasn't about or there would have been ructions. Ach now Danny she is some machine, leather seats, mahogney dash and the heat inside her wasn't ordinary. Speaking with a English accent, he was well, at the start but when he was speaking a while he went back to the same old Martin".

"Edmund was saying he was dressed like a millionaire", Danny replied.

"I never saw the like of it" said Bosco "new suit, shirt and tie, shiny shoes and red socks. The jewellery dripping off him, watch, rings, a bangle sort of thing, and a hankie in his breast pocket. Smoking a big cigar he was. He did admit the car was just half paid for and it would be Christmas before he'd be finished paying for it. By that time he says it'll probably be time to change. I'd say he'll be calling with you sometime soon for he's wild to show off this car".

"How long is he home for"? questioned Danny. "He's not going back for a fortnight", said Bosco, but he says he's going to Kerry to meet someone who he knew over there. He kinda hinted it was a girl". After a few more minutes discussing Martin they headed for home. On the way Danny was more determined than ever to make an effort to go back with him. "He was never one of my best pals", thought Danny, "he was always too sly but if abody could use him to get established over there, that's all I'd want". Danny had drawn a fairly healthy picture to Bosco about going back to England with Martin.

"Wouldn't it just be brilliant to be able to have all the luxuries Martin has and there's no reason why we couldn't, we're steadier workers than he was when he was here. There's no reason, why we couldn't gather up a few bob from now till March".

Bosco agreed. "It would help in a whole lot of ways, I don't know how Susan would take it."

"Do you know the answer to that problem", said Danny, "take her and Alice with us".

Bosco rubbed his hands" now you're talking, I have a notion Susan would go. If she would it could be a sound move".

After further discussion they decided to investigate the situation more. The big item now would be selling this idea to his parents. Over breakfast he repeated all Bosco had told him about Martin, Granny was still in bed so he didn't have to listen to any slighting of the Carlin clan. His father rose first from the table and as he was leaving he instructed Danny to cycle into the town and bring home medicine for fluke from the chemist.

Tess announced she had promised Mrs Flanagan a dozen eggs so he could deliver them as well, "tidy yourself up a bit and don't be shaming us over the whole country", said Tess.

Danny was about to go up to his room to change his trousers when he heard the noise of a car pull on to the street. It was Martin, as he alighted from the car Danny could see he was still dressed in the fancy outfit Bosco had talked about. "Hello mate" he shouted over to Danny. "How's times?"

"Well not as good as yours anyway", answered Danny. "That's a mighty yoke you're driving".

"Well I always said if I could gather up a few pounds I'd purchase a fairly good car. "Here take a look inside".

Danny went over and sat in the passenger seat, "heavens above, there's not many better than that, well not around these parts anyway". In a broken English accent Martin explained he could purchased a cheaper version but the seats wouldn't have been leather and the dash wouldn't have been walnut. "I worked pretty long hours for three months and was able to pay cash none of that hire purchase crack for me. That damned way would rob you".

Suddenly Danny realised this was a different story than the one he told Bosco. It mystified Danny.

Tess came down the yard with the eggs for Mrs Flanagan. "Hello Martin, your welcome home. My oh! what a great big bus that is, I wouldn't like to be buying petrol to keep her going".

"Well it's like this Mrs Higgins there would be no use in having her unless you could afford to buy fuel to keep her on the road".

"Come on Danny and go to the town, your daddy would expect you back shortly", said Tess. "There's money in the bowl on the dresser for the medicine, I must go and dig a few spuds for the dinner. " It's good to see you Martin, I'm sure we'll see you again before you go back".

"No doubth Mrs Higgins", answered Martin. "You never got yourself any wheels of your own yet Danny"?

"Nothing more than a two wheeler which has to be peddled", answered Danny.

"I'm going towards the town, why don't you come in with me. It'll be much easier than pushing a bike up those hills", Martin remarked.

"OK then", said Danny. "I wouldn't mind a spin in the Ford, come into the house I'll be ready in a couple of minutes". They both went into the house and Danny heads to his bedroom to change his clothes. As Martin took a seat he heard a shuffling noise behind him. It was granny.

"Hello Mrs Higgins", said Martin nervously, your still hale and hearty I see, great to see you so well" "Oh aye sure you didn't hear anyone over there saying I'd died", questioned Granny. Martin remembered that she always had a sarcastic way with her. Even his father often remarked how she could cut you to the bone with a few words.

"I'm running Danny into the town in the car", said Martin.

"Oh you've a car have you"? asked Granny. "I suppose you'd need one over in England. It would be hard to thumb a lift all the time".

"That's right", said Martin. "Everyone over there has their own transport it's not like here".

"Then of course they buy everything on the easy payment system", said Granny, not like here we don't purchase anything unless we have money to pay for it. "I'm sure the payments would be big on that boat".

Martin let a nervous giggle "They're not too bad, I manage".

Granny goes over and eases herself into her chair "I'm killed with these pains", said Granny. "But I suppose I'm at an age something will come along to kill me. You don't have any pains yet Martin"? Granny asked. "Mind you, your father and grandfather both had bad backs. I remember Dan got your father to help him one spring but his back give out after about three hours into the first day. He went home and stayed in bed for a week or so, poor man. He had to send your mother over for his wages for the three hours".

"He got that back from lifting heavy items when he was young", said Martin, "he used to warn us to make sure and lift nothing heavy".

"Well there you are now", answered Granny, "its good advice I hope you stick to it".

"I try my best", said Martin.

"I'm sure you do", granny replied sarcastically.

Danny come down and went to lift the money out of the bowl, "Four shillings", he said angrily. That's just enough for the medicine. I told ma I needed money for a new tyre for my bike, it's completely done".

"Don't worry", said Martin. "I'll lend you the price of the tyre, sure it's only a few pence altogether". Granny shuffled in her chair saying. "You'll do nothing of the kind here Danny take what you want out of my purse".

Danny was surprised at this development and took a ten shilling note from the purse. "Thanks granny and if I have any change I'll bring it back to you".

"Hold on to it, it was never known a Higgins had to be bailed out by anyone", said Granny. The two boys left for the town, after a while Tess come in with the potatoes. "Were you talking to Martin, granny", Tess asked. "I hope you didn't insult him".

"Well! I don't think I did, or at least he didn't realise it if I did. As they made the journey to the town Danny quizzed Martin about life in London. Martin explained jobs was very easily found. "I changed jobs nearly every week when I went over first. I love the job I'm in now", said Martin. I'm more or less my own boss I drive from site to site making sure the work is on time. My boss and I get on fine. He treats me well but then I suppose he has to, you see his second daughter Irene has a mighty crush on me. The only drawback, she hinting about getting married and I'm not that keen. You know I think there's time enough, I'd like to play the field if you know what I mean".

"I suppose there any amount of girls over there", asked Danny.

"Ah ha! Loads of them explained Martin and you don't have to ask them out, they do that for you. As well, they're not like the girls around here, if you get a watery kiss off them, your doing well. No, if you leave a girl home over there she expects you to stay the night.

Martin pointed out to Danny most weekends he'd spend at a race meeting or sometimes at Spurs home ground White Hart Lane. "You see Irene's father has a corporate box. We'd often spent all of Saturday there", said Martin. They bring you food, drink, the lot. Then Irene and I would hit the sack, no questions asked, it's a long way from playing football for Kickhams through muck and cowsdung and riding a aul rusty bike three mile home in a downpour".

Danny remarked he had heard that his brother Owenie was going back with him.

"Aye I told him he would be a fool if he didn't. I could set him up in a job the very first day" said Martin "he would do well over there. I know he doesn't work much here but when he opens a well filled pay packet every week he'll be mad keen. I remember gathering spuds for Frank Blaney we worked to long after dark, three days and at the end of it he slipped me a ten shilling note and stood and looked at me as much as to say, am I generous or what. Ten bloody shillings for three long days. That would put anybody from working".

After reaching the town Danny made his way to the chemist to purchase the medicine. Then he made his way up to Sweeny's bicycle shop to get the tyre, as he was about to leave he was Martin talking to Susan Friel, Bosco's girlfriend through the car window. He drew back into the shop for a while looking at a few new bicycles. He pretended he was interested in purchasing one. He talked at length to Terry Sweeney about the price of them, finishing off by saying he'd talk it over with his father. As he exited the shop he pretended he was counting change. He wanted to give Susan time to move away for he was quite sure she wouldn't want him to know she was talking to Martin. The trick worked, when he finally looked up he could see her disappear around the corner at the other end of Main Street.

"I'll never let on I saw anything", he thought, "just to see if Martin mentions their conversation".

He didn't. All the way home Martin still relayed to Danny the fine lifestyle he had in England. "I couldn't live here now, he announced, as a matter of fact I'm missing the danged place already. I have a great notion I'll head back in the next few days. The only draw back is, my cousin from Longford is expecting a lift back. He came home with me".

Danny thought this way the right time to tell him he was thinking of going to England. "Myself and Bosco is thinking of going over for a few months now in the winter time", said Danny. "We could come back again in the spring time when the farm becomes busy".

Martin didn't answer right away and Danny could see he was flustered. "Well I suppose why not" said Martin. "All I'll say is in spring or summer work is handier found". He then changed the subject rather quickly.

As Danny was leaving the car he decided to test him again. "I'll talk to you in the next few days about travelling", said Danny. "First of all I'd have to talk it over with Bosco and the aul pair. The other thing is if we went over with you we'd make out on our own right away, we wouldn't like to think we'd burden anyone".

"That was something I wanted to mention to you", said Martin. "I mightn't be in the position to help you. With Owenie coming over things could become crowded but my cousin Gerry for Longford will probably get you fixed up with jobs and digs. I'm going down to see him in a day or so and I'll tell him of your intentions. I'd say your mum and dad won't be overly happy at you moving out". As he watched the car speed off he had a feeling Martin wasn't overly happy about his proposal.

The next morning at the crossroads Danny relayed all to Bosco. "I thought by him he wasn't very enthusiastic about us going", said Danny.

"Hold on a minute", answered Bosco. "I don't think the boss will let me go, I'll have to approach the subject very gently or I'll get a graip stuck in my backside".

"Oh! I nearly forgot to tell you", said Danny, when I came out of Sweeney's the bicycle shop I saw your Susan talking to Martin through the car window I pretended I didn't see her and when I reached the car she had vanished, I was waiting on Martin to say he was chatting to her but not a cheep".

"That bloody edgit and his fancy car will upset all the girls in the country", moaned Bosco. They thyrsted to meet at the crossroads that evening and see if developments had advanced any.

Both arrived that evening and Bosco had bad news about his emigration plans. Sometime during the day he hinted to his father he was thinking of going back with Martin to England.

"He glared at me for what seemed a long while", said Bosco. "What in the name of Jayus would you be going to England for"? he asked. I said to look for work. He says "look for work, look for work, you stay here you lazy hoor ye and you'll not have to look for work for I'll make sure you'll have as much of it as you can cope with". He had a bucket in his hand and he sent it whizzing past my ear. "Don't let me hear you at such shite again and off he walked still ranting and raving".

"So you won't be going I take it", queried Danny. "Bloody right I won't", answered Bosco. "But maybe it's for the best the relationship between me and Susan is getting quite serious and I don't know if I'd be happy at not seeing her for six months".

Danny announced he still hadn't mentioned the plan to any of his parents and he knew it probably wouldn't go down well.

"The only thing I can say", said Danny, "they'll not use violence to stop me from going". They saw a car coming in the distance and they recognised it right away as Martins. "Here", said Danny, "we'll hide in behind the hedge until he passes for I heard enough boasting from that buck yesterday to do me for weeks.

Martin's car drove past very slowly, both Danny and Bosco had a clear view and both of they gasped at what they saw. Beside Martin in the front was Susan and Martins brother Owenie and Alice sat in the back.

"Did you see that did you"? Bosco asked.

"I sure did", answered Danny.

Bosco now half crying said "The sly wee witch, look what she's done on me and him the prick with all these girlfriends in England and he has to come home and steal the only girl I had a fondness for".

"As well as that", said Danny. "Did you notice how slowly he drove past the crossroads he probably thought we would be standing about so he could blow the horn at us".

Bosco was now in an agitated state and suggested they should confront him. But Danny pointed out he had no interest in Alice anymore and still hoping to travel to England with Martin he thought its best to keep out of it.

"I think the best plan would be when you meet Susan tomorrow ask her what's she playing at", advised Danny. After all it's as much her fault as Martin's. Anyway maybe it's all innocent enough, just bringing them for a drive".

After a lot of discussion Danny eventually convinced Bosco that he would be better confront Susan and let her explain her case. As both of them headed home their different ways Danny smiled at the thought of Bosco's father almost hitting him with a bucket, and wondered what would happen if Bosco announced he was going to marry Susan any time soon. When he entered the house he could see his mother was alone, granny had gone to bed and Dan was away ceilidhing in a neighbour's house. "Now", thought Danny, "this is as good a time as any to bring up the subject of going back with Martin. He made himself a cup of tea. "Ma", he said, "what I'm going to say now I'm sure you'll not particular like, but myself and Bosco are thinking about going to England for a few months, you know over the winter".

His mother left down the garment she was patching, she let a nervous giggle. "I don't know what it was something told me you might think like that", she said. "You haven't been settled right since that episode with Emma, then Martin arrived like a millionaire, I had a feeling it would unsettle you more". There was a brief silence as she groped for the right words to say "Ach Danny we would rather you didn't", she continued. "I know things are changing and your young and you want to have things that we can live well without, but ...... your father isn't getting any younger he needs you to help him around the place".

"But ma it would only be for the winter months, we will be back again in the Spring, say March to help put the crops in" argued Danny. "I'd have a few pounds home with me that I could do something with that would make all our lives a bit easier".

"That's fine in theory but what happens if you like it over there and wants to stay", said Tess, "in a few years time we'll be a rare looking set here alone".

"No, it wouldn't be like that", said Danny. "You know I wouldn't abandon you like that". "Away to your bed", said Tess, and give this serious consideration before you do anything. I'll find out what your father thinks about the whole thing, although I know exactly what he'll think about it".

Tess brought up his notion of leaving anytime her and Danny were alone. She said Dan was not at all pleased with his proposal. Danny told her Bosco had decided not to go. He didn't explain to her that he'd only implicated Bosco to make his case more acceptable. Then one day as they had a rest out in the fields where they were working, his father asked him if he was serious about leaving. Danny said it was true and done his best to explain his reasons behind it. He found it much harder to talk about it to his father compared to his mother. A long silence developed which was broken up by his father telling a story about when he was Danny's age.

"Me and Colm O Sullivan were big pals", he explained, "we went everywhere together, then we got talking one night about going over to his uncle in England, we made big plans but I knew I had a mighty task on my hands to convince my mother. Of course my father dead I was the only help she had. Then one night when I thought I'd my plan well worked out I put my proposal to her. She immediately started to cry saying she'd have to sell that farm, the place that my father had worked himself to death over. She invited the parish priest out to talk to me, he become quite angry and in the end made me kneel down and swear I'd put such thoughts out of my head. As well she had a brother who went to America and wasn't heard of for years and when they did it was because he was killed in a brawl in Chicago bar. He hadn't a penny to his name. In the end I just told Colm that I couldn't go, I still remember how disappointed I was. Colm went ahead and done well for himself. After he bought a lot of property around Birmingham".

After another fairly long pause he added "I would hate to see you go Danny but if you did go I'd hope you'd keep your promise and come home again in the spring, but think it through it mightn't be all sunshine over there.

Danny gave a sigh of relief, he felt his father with his teenage experience understood his longing to better himself so he decided more or less right away he could now make sturdy plans to make the move happen.

CHAPTER 18

The next morning he told Bosco he was going for sure. Again he tried to coax Bosco to join him but without success. As well as his father's bad temper, he felt now he couldn't live without Susan in his life and she wasn't interested in his suggestion of going with him.

"She didn't think much of you when she went swanning about with Martin in that big car", said Danny.

"She explained all that to me", answered Bosco. "Martin was taking Owenie, his brother and Alice for a run and Susan went along as well, no strings attached. They came out this way so Martin could show Susan my homestead. She was very annoyed when I confronted her about it. She said I was the only guy for her and she was hoping in not too distant the future we could get engaged".

Danny decided the next time he met Martin he would tell him he was travelling back with him. A night or so later when they were alone he told his mother his mind was made up, he was going. She told him she was disappointed but she wished him the best of luck. As he rose to go to bed she grabbed him and give him a big hug. Danny could feel her warm tears spilling on his cheek, as he headed towards the door, looking back he could see she was sitting bent over crying. A few days later he met Martin and told him of his plan. Martin wasn't overly delighted and questioned Danny if he was doing the right thing. He would be leaving behind a fairly comfortable life style and then he had his football which he might miss more than he might expect. Reluctantly Martin promised he wouldn't see him stuck.

"We're going back this day week", said Martin. "I will be away most of next week for I've a girl to see down in Galway and I'll be calling with Gerry, my cousin on my back up. I'll let you know what time I'll lift you". One night a while after Tess had told Granny, she confronted him, "Heavens above what's wrong with your head, haven't you everything here you want, spoilt rotten you are, listening to that Carlin buck boasting. You might find out you could be much better off than he is with all his fancy clothes and big car".

"It's only for a few months to the spring comes around", answered Danny. I'll be back again and by that time I'll have found out what the place is like at least". Every morning that week Danny and Bosco met at the crossroads, even though he was excited about going part of him knew he'd miss the morning chats with Bosco. That Friday evening Martins sister arrived over and told him he'd be lifted the next day at three o'clock. That morning himself and Bosco had a long discussion.

"You're a lucky bloody man", announced Bosco, "getting away from this dull dump. Nothing but work and nothing much for it. You'll write and tell me all about it and who knows I could join you at some stage".

On the morning he was leaving the two met as usual at the crossroads. The mood was pretty sombre and Danny was wishing he didn't have all the goodbyes to go through.

"Well lad", said Bosco, "this is it for a while, I know for sure I'll miss you big time, be sure and write and it'll not be overly long to the springtime altogether".

"It'll fly in", said Danny. "Blink and it'll be Christmas, blink again it'll be St Patricks Day. Here Bosco take this I'll purchase another one over there". He takes the wee transistor radio from his pocket and gives it to Bosco. "What the hell are you doing"? asked Bosco. "Hold on to it yourself".

"No, I want you to have it", said Danny, "something to remind me by. "Ach! your too decent, said Bosco. Although it was the next thing I was going to purchase out of Cassie Byrnes catalogue".

They shook hands. "Look after yourself Danny", said Bosco. He turned and walked away without looking back.

With a hour to go before he was lifted Danny finished getting dressed, his mother was packing his case. Danny wished the next hour or so was over. He knew there would be a few tears shed. He hated to see the folks sad especially his mother for no matter how hard he tried to convince them it was only for a short while, they still looked upon this as unnecessary. He was disturbed from his thoughts by his granny calling him. She was still in bed for she wasn't feeling that well the past few days.

"Are you all set", she asked.

"I think so granny but I'll be away so short a time I'll manage somehow", said Danny. "It mightn't be for long but I have a feeling you will not see me alive again" said Granny.

"Ach! hold your tongue granny, of course I will", answered Danny. He quoted again what he'd said to Bosco "blink and it will be Christmas, blink again and it'll be St Patricks Day and I will be arriving home again".

"I hope your right", said Granny, "but I feel my spirits are fading fast. "Here take this, it's a wee bit I saved from my pension". She handed him a small bundle of notes.

"No Granny", Danny began.

"Take it, it isn't much but you could be doing with it", argued Granny. I wouldn't want you borrowing from your man Carlin".

Danny could feel himself welling up inside He took the money and reached down and gave Granny a gentle hug, the first since he was about six years of age.

"Thanks Granny", he whispered. She reached under her pillow and brought out a pair of rosary beads. "Take these as well and keep them with you day and night and they'll save you from danger".

"But I can't take those granny, they are the ones that Mammy brought back from Knock for you last year. I know you place a lot of value on them".

"Take them I say", said Granny, and use them every day". We're going to miss you so much Danny I'm not sure how your mum and dad will cope. I'll miss you as well. Many a battle me and you had but at the end of the day we're of the same stalk, God bless you".

Danny made his way down to the kitchen "I think I've all in", said Tess. I put in a note pad with Maggie Duffins phone number, I asked her would it be alright if you rang when you arrived tomorrow. She was delighted and said she bring over the message herself as soon as she got it. Oh! I nearly forgot, last night Edmund gave your father a pound note to give you. Here take it and put it with the rest and make sure to keep it in a safe place".

Again, Danny was overwhelmed "Good lord that was a huge surprise".

"Well we tried to tell you he wasn't all bad", answered his mother.

"Where's da?" asked Danny "I haven't seen him about this while".

"Your daddy said it would be better if he wasn't about when you were leaving", said Tess. "He told me to tell you he wished you luck and he'll be looking forward to the springtime when he sees you again".

"Holy heavens I didn't think I'd have that impact on him", said Danny.

He never thought it would be so hard, then he heard the noise of the car coming up the lane. As it pulled up at the door Danny could see there was only one fella in the car and seeing he didn't know him he surmised it was Gerry O'Grady from Longford, Martin's cousin. Gerry introduced himself as did Danny.

"Where's Martin?" asked Danny.

"He has still a few things to see to so he's staying for a few more days", answered Gerry.

"It's good of him to give you the car", said Danny.

"Aye", answered Gerry dryly.

"Maybe if I go up to the top of the yard and give a shout Daddy might be about", remarked Danny.

"You'd only be wasting your time, he'll not be appearing", said Tess.

The moments were getting more awkward "Well", said Gerry. "I'll put in your suitcase and you can say your goodbyes".

"You'll keep him right until he finds his feet", said Tess. "Indeed I will", assured Gerry. "I've been told you're a good worker and there's plenty of it to be done where we're going. If you work hard you'll earn good money and if you don't like it over there as many an Irishman didn't, no harm done, you can come home".

"Thanks", said Tess.

Danny goes to the bedroom and bids goodbye to Granny in almost silence "Come home safe to us", granny said as he left.

"Right ma, I'll ring Duffins when we arrive", said Danny.

Tess burst out crying and threw her arms around him "Please mammy don't cry its only making it harder for me It's only for a short time".

There was another fella told me that before but……" blurted Tess. As he made for the door he whispered "I promise". Gerry had went up the yard and turned the car and was now waiting for him, as he opened the car door he felt something rub against his leg, it was Jip the dog. His tail wagging looking up at him with his innocent eyes oblivious to what was going on. He had kept his emotions in check but this was the last straw, his tears poured out of him.

"You can't come today Jip", said Danny, closing the car door. He didn't put down the car window, just waved out and Gerry gently eased the car forward. As they climbed the bray looking back he could see his mother moving towards the door. Gerry said nothing, he knew silence was probably best for a few moments until Danny composed himself. High up, in the far hill in the shadow of a sycamore tree stood a lonely figure following the progress of the car as it climbed the bray and made its way a long the straight road until it finally disappeared. Dan wiped his eyes and began to trudge down towards the house "May God look after you son", he whispered to himself.

Danny broke the silence. "I wonder what Martin had still to do after being at home for a fortnight. It was danged good of him to lend you his car to go back".

Gerry let a giggle. "His car", he announced. "I'm afraid this isn't Martins car. It's a car I hired for the fortnight. He dropped me off with the understanding he'd drop it down to me the next day or so. Eight days were gone before I saw it".

"Oh! the bugger", explained Danny, he told us it was his and he had it almost paid for and then he was purchasing even a better one".

"That would be Martin alright", said Gerry. "I suppose he told you he was making fantastic money".

"He did indeed", said Danny. "He said he was working for a millionaire and courting his only daughter".

"Martin hasn't worked the last four months he as there", said Gerry. "Before that we went from job to job often only staying a few days, then he would lie up in the flat often for a week or two. I was pretty fed up with him, I had no intention of coming home but I decided I'd bring him home and leave him there, a bloody fraud if there was ever one".

"And the flashy suit and jewellery I suppose that was a big front", said Danny.

"Of course", answered Gerry. "The whole lot cost about fifteen pounds, borrowed off me".

"I just can't understand him said Danny, the fibs he has told us. He definitely fooled everybody around home"

"He fooled the landlady too", said Gerry, pretending he had a sore back, he told her if he could make it home his father would pay for an operation but the doctors in England warned him to be careful. One wrong twist and he'd be paralysed for life. She provided him with meals and charged him no rent for the last four months. It would have done you good seeing her arming him out to the car the day we come home".

"I'll not make her any wiser, I'll tell her he's already had his operation and it was an great success", Danny replied.

Danny and Gerry seemed to hit it off and was enjoying each other's company, Gerry filled Danny in on how things worked in London. There's a good living to be made and plenty of opportunities to better one self.

Gerry assured Danny he would have him working almost immediately "I know one or two fellas who's crying out for a willing man". They sailed overnight and journeyed the next day to London, dropped off the car with the rental firm and took a train to their digs. Gerry had lined out the arrangement of the digs on the boat over.

"The landlady is very accommodating when it comes to meals and such things", Gerry assured Danny.

When they arrived at the house he saw right away what he meant. She fussed over them and insisted she'd make them a fry. Gerry explained to her, Vonnie Murray, Danny's connection to Martin.

"Their mothers are full cousins", he lied.

"If your half as pleasant as Martin you'll do fine", she replied. "And the poor fellow crippled with a bad back". Danny had already told Gerry he was to phone Duffin's when he arrived so Maggie could contact his mother. Gerry dialled the number and when the phone was answered he left Danny to speak and give Maggie the message that he'd arrived safely and was in good hands. Later on in the evening he heard Gerry on the phone and when he arrived back in the room he announced he had already secured him a job.

"It's with two fellas who lay kerbs and paving, Terry and Noel Morgan. "They are actually cousins of mine also, on my father's side from Roscommon, they'll be lifting you tomorrow morning at seven O'clock outside the Red Lion pub", explained Gerry, "If you want any work clothes or boots you can take a loan of Martin's, they're there in the wardrobe, you'll find they haven't taken much wear".

"This is it", thought Danny.

He could feel the excitement building and much apprehension not knowing what to expect. After he went to bed he found it hard to sleep, with the noise of constant traffic on top of all else. His thoughts turned to home. Edmund Coyle was probably over on his ceilidhe. He usually would call on Sunday night. Bosco would probably have taken Susan to the pictures. He wondered how the Blues fared against

St Pats in today's game. Somewhere midst of it all he must have fallen asleep. What seemed as only minutes Gerry was nudging him.

LET THE "FUTURE" BEGIN

"Come on Danny rise and shine, its quarter past six, we can't have you being late on your first day".

Gerry's workmate Simon came and lifted them in the van.

Gerry explained to Danny what would happen. "We will drop you off at The Red Lion. It's a pub at an intersection where men wait for their lifts to work", explained Gerry. "Here wear this" Gerry handed Danny a black woollen cap. "It might seem odd to wear a woollen cap and the weather so hot but it's just that Terry, my cousin will recognise you. You can take it off in his van". After about ten minutes they arrived at the Red Lion.

The place was buzzing. "Right then", said Gerry, "stand about there, Terry will be along shortly, see you tonight".

Danny took up a position near a wall there was men everywhere large men small men, young, old, all sorts. The streets were already busy with traffic. Some of the men were singing, others were sitting on their hunkers silent and looking the worse of the wear. A few were shouting across at each other something to do with work. New members were arriving steady, then a wicked argument broke out between two. It became very heated. Danny guessed it was over work the previous week. It all became very vicious as both men started to punch each other, screaming into each other faces. Two men tried to calm the protagonists down but they weren't having it. The bigger of the two pushed the smaller man out on to the street. A motorist had to brake hard to avoid him. He started to yell at the men. The bigger one reached in and tried to pull the driver out through the window. The smaller man was kicking the car. A policeman directing traffic arrived over. Instead of calming the situation he made things worse. Others started shouting at the policeman. Eventually he walked away.

New men arrived, some carrying toolboxes, others carrying a lunch box.

"Holy jaysus", thought Danny. What a bloody kip". All of a sudden he felt very homesick. All this commotion wasn't to his liking. His mind started to wondered to home, he looked at the time, five past seven.

"Daddy would just be up by now", he thought. He had always the same routines every morning summer or winter. He'd let Jip out, then he'd check the cows, in the winter in the byre, summer time out in the field. He'd then light the fire, fill and hang on the kettle. Then he'd kneel down and say his prayers, Tess would now arrive down from the bedroom and Dan would fill her in about the type of weather outside. When the kettle was boiled she called Danny and have the tea and a slice of bread on the table for him. Then he'd follow his father to the byre to milk the cows by hand, it was so peaceful.

Another row broke out, something about wages, a van had pulled up, a large burley fellow ascended from the van and confronted a smaller man.

"If you want work that's what you're getting paid, take it or leave it", said the van driver.

"Go be damned", said the small fella "you're not going to have me for a slave anymore". His lunchbox was on the pavement beside him, the big fella drew his foot off it sending the contents out on to the road.

"Stay there you hoor", he shouted.

He came over to Danny "Hi son, are you looking for a day's work".

Danny was caught unawares, he looked blankly at the man. He thought this might be the man Gerry had arranged to lift him.

"Ah jaysus lad are you a bloody dummy, do you want work"? "No, no, said Danny. I'm being lifted".

"Good luck to your employer, he has a quare lively creature when he has you", said the man as he moved away.

The only place Danny wanted to be just then was back at home milking the big black cow. Listening to the rhythm of the milk strones as they hit the bucket. He decided there and then this situation wasn't for him. The whole affair was a big mistake. He started to plan what he would do, he'd tell Terry and Noel he wasn't going, then he'd get a taxi to bring him back to the digs. When Gerry would arrive home he'd explain this wasn't for him and Gerry could instruct him the best way to get home. He was sorting it out in his head if he'd have enough money to bring him home when he got a tap on the shoulder and a pleasant looking fellow was standing there.

"Have I got the right man, your Danny", he asked. Danny nodded. "Sorry we're a bit late, jump in" as he opened the van door.

The driver shook hands with Danny, "Please to meet you Danny, I'm Terry", he said. "That's a dire place on a Monday morning, but your alright now we'll see you come to no harm".

They travelled for about forty minutes, most of the talk centred on, Getting to know you questions. He found out these men were in England for around seven years. Noel was married and Terry was single. They hailed from Wexford.

"Life can be good here", maintained Terry. "But go the wrong way about it and it can be cruel, damned cruel".

They travelled along crowded streets, narrow side streets, over big bridges and down a duel carriageway.

"You seemed to know your way about", said Danny, they both laughed.

"When we come over first", said Noel, we were mesmerised how anyone could get to know this place but when you have to you soon learn".

They eventually pulled up at a large building site. It turned out to be an new shopping complex, they were greeted by a few other tradesmen as they made their way through an entry to where they'd been working the week before. A tall red haired man came over.

"Ah a new recruit", he said. "We'll see things speeding up now. When he left Terry said "That's the foreman, not a bad lad but don't get him angered".

Noel then told Danny what they wanted him to do. He was to wheel sand in a barrow through the narrow entry and tip it beside where they were laying the pavers. Then when he had so much sand they'd told him to bring a few barrows of pavers.

After a while Noel told Danny to slow down and take it easy or they'd have a build up of sand. "You'll soon get to know yourself when we need sand and also know where to tip it".

Everything was falling into place, he soon got the hang of it. Now and again men would pass by and make comments mostly about Danny or "The new fella" as they called him. Danny had paid no attention to the time but when he looked at his watch he was surprised, it was still not nine O'clock.

"Holy heavens", he thought. "I could have sworn we were working four hours or more".

Every now and then he'd glance at his watch and think back to what would be happening at home, Dan would have finished the milking by now", he thought. "I don't suppose he'll wait for Bosco at the crossroads".

As the day wore on Danny started to think what he'd do, stay or head back home again, after toing and froing, he made up his mind, he'd stay a couple of weeks and if he wasn't pretty settled by then he'd go home. The day trudged by, the work though not overly hard, was constant. He was glad when the days work was over and they headed for home. Noel dropped him off at his digs and told him he'd lift him there at ten to seven the next morning.

The landlady had his dinner ready as soon as he had his clothes changed and himself washed. As he sat down at the table Gerry came in through the door. He was anxious to know how Danny fared and was pleased when Danny assured all went well.

The landlady fussed over the two of them "It's easy to see you are a cousin of Martins" she announced. "You have the same easy way of going on and like him, you've delightful manners". Danny got it hard to keep in the laughing when he looked over at Gerry. After dinner Danny decided to write home. He purchased a writing pad, envelope and a pen at the near hand corner shop. As he sat down in his bedroom to write a fierce loneliness came over him. He wished he could stroll up to the crossroads with Jip and meet Bosco. Monday evening there was plenty to discuss after the weekend, football, films, dances. There usually would be a fight to comment on, maybe at the football or at a dance. Jip would have his usual run chasing the hare, who seemed to enjoy torturing him. He looked around the small bedroom "So this is it" he thought. Gerry was contently reading a paper in the sitting room as he passed the door. Even listening to Edmund Coyle telling long winded stories or having a yarn with Johney the spade on the road would have been welcomed. He slowly made himself comfortable and started his letter "Dear Ma and Da", he consecrated a while before he went any further.

He knew what he would have liked to say " Ma, will you bake a scone of my favourite treacle bread for I'll be home tonight"

No, he would have to be careful and make sure he didn't write anything that would give them an inkling of how he felt. Best he thought to keep it short and upbeat. He told them he had his first working day over him. He explained the kind of work he was doing and how the two men he was working for, Terry and Noel were very easy going and good craic. He told them about the landlady and how much she fussed over himself and Gerry, and her believing he was a first cousin of Martin Carlins. "She seemed to have a soft spot for Martin" he said then he relayed the news Gerry had told about the fraud that Martin was. "It's strange at the moment with the busy streets and all but when I get I know my way about better it'll be fine". He finished by saying he was looking forward to getting a letter and hearing all the news from home. He read it through a few times to make sure they wouldn't guess he was terribly homesick. The landlady had told him she would post it the next morning. Around nine o'clock she made them all tea and biscuits and by ten Gerry and himself were in bed. It had been a traumatic day over all. That morning outside the Red Lion was a nightmare and through the day the constant noise was hard to get used too.

A few nights after Danny left, just before Tess and Dan went to bed, Tess left down the garment she was mending.

"There's something has been puzzling me Dan, I thought you would have made a bigger objection over Danny leaving. You seemed to accept it very mildly".

Dan didn't speak for a little while. "Well, the reason I didn't kick up much of a fuss goes back when I was Danny's age or a few years older. I was friendly with a fella Colm OSullivan. He had an uncle who owned a bar in Birmingham. This man wasn't married and was pushing on in years, so he asked Colm to come over and help him to run. Colm asked me if I'd like to go as his uncle had hinted another hand wouldn't go wrong. We spent night after night planning the whole venture. I was determined to go, to see what the place was like, just like Danny. I knew there'd be stiff opposition from my mother, after all I was the only help she had. One night, not long before the departure day I picked up courage and told her of my plans. She was very calm about her whole affair I couldn't believe it.

The next day was a Sunday and we just had our dinner eaten when who arrived only Father Lynch. Well he was roaring at the top of his voice before he reached the front door. He didn't say hello or anything, just a continuous barrage, his face bright red. He came over lifted me off the chair I was sitting at the table by the collar, now my face was level with his.

"Have you no respect for this poor woman after all she's done for you".

He kept ranting and raving for what seemed like an hour. He covered everything, I'd put her in an early grave. The farm would have to be sold, could I have that on my conscience for the rest of my life. Before he finished he introduced hell. That's where I was going. He stopped, looked over at my mother.

She cleared her throat "Father Lynch is right", that's all she said.

What could I do only to say I wouldn't be leaving. "Now", said Father Lynch, we'll kneel down and say the rosary for thanks giving. I remember how disappointed and bitter I was. Colm went on to Birmingham and in no time his uncle gave him the bar. He ended up with several pubs over there. That's why my opposition to Danny leaving was weak. I didn't want him to feel as disappointed as I was".

After a few seconds Tess asked, "Colm OSullivan, that was the small ginger haired fellow with a squeaky voice".

"That was him", Dan replied. "We were very close. A bit like Danny and Bosco".

Again Tess didn't speak for a few moments "There was rumour's that it was him and another fella that took Kitty Doogans gate and hid it".

"Maybe", was all Dan said.

Tess stirred in the chair "I'm going to ask you something Dan and I'd hope you'd tell me the truth, were you the other lad"?

"It's a long time ago", answered Dan.

"Yes it is", said Tess. "But that's not an honest answer to the question. Was it you"?

Dan took a while to answer. "We didn't mean any harm. The young ones always have done tricks like that around Halloween even to this day. Didn't some jokers take Edmunds feeding throg from the field below the road last year and tied it high up on a tree. He had some bother getting it down again. I wouldn't misdoubt it was our boy and Bosco were the culprits".

"All the same would it not have been the decent thing to own up to it", enquired Tess. "Instead Leo Burke was accused of a crime he didn't commit". Again Dan was hesitant "Nobody accused him of it only Father Lynch. There was friction between the two of them for a long while before what happened at the dance. One Sunday about a year before Father Lynch came around by the chapel as second Mass was being said and caught Leo and Willie Corr standing outside. He started to roar at them to get inside. Willie went into the chapel but Leo stood his ground and defied Father Lynch. The next Sunday he preached from the altar and left no one in doubt who he was calling a heathen and blasphemer.

"Isn't it ironic that after years of bad mouthing Leo, little does your mother know it was her son who caused poor Kitty's death". Tess rose, went to the door "So you two said nothing I wouldn't have thought that very brave". Opening the door she left and wandered down the lane with her thoughts of how all turned out and how much different it could have been.

CHAPTER 19

The following days weren't much different from the first one. Every evening he'd walk down to the corner shop and buy something, normally a bar of chocolate. One evening he decided to explore further. He could see some distance away an entrance to a park. The daylight was completely gone so went as far as the gates. There were quite a few people out walking with dogs. He sat down on a bench just inside the gate and watched as people sauntered by. He couldn't tell how big the park was because it vanished away in the distance. "I'll explore more of it" he thought before the evenings become too dark. As they were taking their tea before bedtime he mentioned to the landlady.

"Oh yes she said, it's a fine big park with plenty of path flowers and shrubs. Most Sundays myself and Margie from next door would go for walks around it".

The following evenings he spent almost an hour travelling further until he had covered it all. Noel asked him later in the week if he was fine about working on Saturday.

"Why not", he replied. I haven't anything better to do". As he was getting out of the van on Saturday, Noel gave him a brown envelope.

"Don't spend it all at the one time", he joked. Danny wasn't really expecting a pay packet until the following week. He had often heard building workers talk about a lying week. As soon as he went up to his room to change he opened the envelope. He started to count the money and his eyes kept widening. Twenty four pounds, he couldn't believe it.

"He's made a mistake", he thought. "Twenty four pounds, I never handled money like this before".

He sat on the bed filled with excitement. Back at home a good tradesman wouldn't be paid any more than eight pounds for a six day week.

"Here am I being paid three times as much", he thought.

He heard Gerry come up the stairs so he was waiting for him on the landing.

"When do we pay the landlady"? he asked Gerry.

"You must have got paid", said Gerry. "Are you happy enough with what you've got".

"I'm over the moon", answered Danny. "I wasn't expecting half of it".

"Well I phoned Noel last night", said Gerry, and he is very pleased with you so I know he'd probably pay you well. Yes I usually paid Vonnie after dinner tonight. Look its none of my business but even though you've surplus, don't go throwing your money around you, it mightn't always be as plenty full".

"Thanks, said Danny, I don't intend to".

He couldn't wait until he would write home the following week and tell his parents how much he was earning. He'd also be able to tell them would send some home in a few week's time. Gerry asked him later on if he wanted to go down to an Irish club.

"I'd normally go down most Saturday nights".

Danny declined the offer saying he was fairly tired but promised he'd travel next Saturday. On Tuesday of the following week a letter from his mother arrived. He couldn't believe how excited he was, wanting to hear all the happenings around home.

Dear Danny,

It's good to hear from you and find you've seemed to have settled in quite well. Your lodgings seem to be quite good and it must help to have Gerry with you, he seems very sensible. If it's to your advantage with the landlady just keep pretending you're a first cousin of Martins. Martin seems to be lying low as no one has seen him since you left. Your father started cutting the corn yesterday. Bosco come over and gave a hand. Daddy asked Johnny the spade to help as well. If the weather stays fine we should have it cleared up by the weekend. Bosco had a lot of questions to ask about your work and all. Maybe you could drop him a line soon. He was telling us the team got beaten by two points on Sunday and everyone was of the opinion if you had been there they'd would have won for sure. Granny isn't too good this week, stayed in bed most of the time but improved a bit yesterday. The only other news around here Cathal McCadden was caught by the water baliffs on the river the other night, he'll be in trouble as this is his third time. I'll close now, I'm sure you must go to bed early seeing you've such a early start. Your loving mother.

P.S Jip has searched everywhere for you. When your father leaves the milk can down in the mornings he always heads up to the crossroads. Bosco says he's still trying to catch that danged old hare, the poor devil doesn't know what's happened to you.

Danny put the letter carefully into the envelope prepared himself and climbed into bed. Once again, not for the first time a terrible loneliness came over him. The excitement of receiving his first pay packet had now reseeded and home sickness had taken its place. He longed to be able to hug Jip and tell him everything was going to be alright. Even to go up to the room and sit on the side of granny's bed and tell her of any news he had. There was no time of the year he liked better than harvest time. With the days getting shorter, gathering in the crops for use all winter, was a special time. His head was in a muddle. Everybody here was more than friendly. The work was no bother to him and of course the pay was a bonus, but for all that, this burning feeling inside his head wouldn't let go.

"Right, he thought. I can't give in just yet, I'll stay another few weeks, a month or so then if things don't improve I'll head back."

At least in his next letter home he can tell them all of the big money he's earning. He kept thinking of the craic himself and Bosco would have had and the banter with Johney the Spade, sleep finally took over. A routine developed, Gerry asked him again if he'd like to go down to the Irish club, the following Saturday night. "There's always some music a drink or so, dancing and a bit of craic. You'd meet people from all parts of Ireland. It's good to know some of them in case you'd happen to be out of work".

So Saturday nights he went with Gerry to the club, at first he just drank orange but after a few weeks he tried a beer. At first he wasn't keen on it but he began to like it some more. On Sundays he went to the local church for mass, after which he had his dinner and usually took a walk in the park. On Sunday night he always wrote a letter home. During the week he often read a book or paper and would retire to bed around 10 o'clock. He told his mother in his second letter of the good wage he was earning.

"After a while I'll send some home", he said. "I want you to find out from someone how to go about having the electric and telephone installed".

He wrote a letter to Bosco not mentioning the bouts of home sickness that often came and could blight a whole day. One week followed another with very little variety. He started to enjoy the club and met the same girls each time and danced them all. He became very popular with everyone down there. He started to enjoy work more with one job completed, they moved to the next one. He was seeing different parts of London. He realised on every job there were a few characters, men who were larger than life. Everyone seemed to latch on to them and have the banter with him. Arguments mostly about football were a regular occurrence. One day someone asked him who did he support and just to give an answer he said Tottenham Hotspurs. From then on he used to follow their progress in the papers. Weeks became months. Every now and then fellas started to talk about making arrangements for going home at Christmas. This would be a good opportunity to pack up and go home. Many nights lying in bed he'd go over his situation. He still hadn't enough money saved to install the electricity and phone, plus buy himself a car. In the end he decided to stick it out for another few months. At least he would be doing what he said he'd do. As the days moved into December all the talk in canteen at work was about the Christmas holidays, some preparing to go home. Others taking a break in some other parts of England or Scotland. He reckoned his holiday was going to be pretty quiet, Noel and Terry were going back home for a fortnight. On Christmas Eve Gerry was travelling to Edinburgh. It was only when he questioned him. Gerry admitted to him he had a girlfriend up there. It struck Danny then this was the reason why he'd gone missing for a few weekends since he came back. It looked like himself and mother Hubbart (Gerry's nickname for the landlady) would be spending a quiet Christmas together, the week before Christmas he opened a bank account, lodged the money he had been saving, receiving a cheque book and sent a cheque home for a hundred pounds. There was a fantastic atmosphere around the club owing to Christmas. On Christmas Eve he brought a food hamper for the landlady, when he presented it to her she gave him a big hug and he could see tears in her eyes.

"Danny, that's too decent of you", she said. "I've been keeping lodgers now for over thirty years and I don't think I had two as decent, well-mannered boys as yourself and Gerry".

"I must say you have been so good to me", answered Danny. "I was telling my mother that here was like home from home".

After he went to bed on Christmas Eve his mind wandered back to Christmas at home. Even though everything was very innocent, there still was a certain buzz around the house. His mother would have reared turkeys for sale and the excitement of procuring a decent price for them. She always baked a few cakes for the festive season. One she'd give to Edmund Coyle. This custom had been going on before she married Dan. She had now for some years baked a cake for Bosco's household. On Christmas Eve Dan would be bringing Edmund his cake while Danny was dispatched to Bosco's house with theirs. Dan would always have home a bottle of whiskey while Bosco's mother would recipicate with a box of biscuits.

Danny's parents always visited the town on Christmas eve as well and came homeladen with gifts from different shops they'd have purchased from all year. A discussion would always take place about which shopkeeper was the most decent. It was during these discussions Granny came into her own.

"So that's all that buck give you", she'd remark. "After all the hard earned money you threw over the counter all year. If I were you I'd cut back on him and give more to your man Dempsey. He gave you twice as much value as that other hungers mother".

His mother always made sure Danny received a fairly good Christmas box, usually some item of clothing. Granny normally would give out about the extragance but at Christmas time she too seemed to be filled with the festive mood. Now as the time neared midnight he visualised what has happening at home. "Granny would have gone to bed a few hours ago" he thought "Mammy would still be fussing preparing the turkey and Daddy would go out as near midnight as possible and give the cows in the byre an extra feed of hay. He remembered asking him why one night. "It was a custom my father had and also his father. "I suppose it was their Christmas box" his Father explained. Everything seemed to be done and dusted just in time for midnight. They all knelt down and said their prayers. Afterwards his mother made tea and biscuits, the last food they'd have until they came from mass in the morning. All seemed so peaceful. A large vehicle rumbled down the street outside he looked at his watch, midnight. "Some poor devil still working". Midnight, a terrible loneliness came over him. What would he not give to be sitting quietly listening to his mother and father making small talk as they drank their tea and biscuits. Tears filled his eyes and spilled down his cheeks, he was weeping more than he ever remembered. After a minute or so there was a gentle knock on the door and the landlady spoke.

"Are you alright Danny?" she asked. He sat up wiped his eyes on his sleeve "Oh! I'm fine", he replied.

He didn't realise he was making any sound.

"Night night see you in the morning", she answered.

He settled in again and somewhere in the night sleep eventually arrived. Christmas and New Year came and went. He visited the Irish Club a few nights and saw in the New Year there. That night he drank more than before and found himself unsteady as he walked home. As he entered the house he tripped on the mat and fell up against a hall table. The landing light came on and the landlady was staring down at him. She didn't say anything out clearly but seemed to mutter to herself. He straightened himself up and made it to his bedroom. The next morning the atmosphere was frosty.

"You seemed to have a lot to drink last night", the landlady said.

"I probably had", answered Danny. "I met quite a few at the club and I didn't realise I had as much until I started to walk home".

"Well just watch yourself", advised the landlady. "Ive seen it all before. After a few months over here and a lot of lads start to drink more than they should and some don't quit until it's too late.

"Sorry", Danny replied.

"I'm not saying it's going to happen to you but just be aware," warned Vonnie.

Danny remembered on the way over on the boat Gerry did mention that the landlady wasn't overly happy about lodgers coming in drunk, so he decided to keep a eye on how much he drank. During his time off he went for long walks and spent a day at the sales in Oxford Street. He was glad when Gerry arrived back and he was able to relate to him all the happenings at the club.

"She gave me my first warning about coming in drunk", he said. "Of course I didn't realise I was intoxicated until I tripped on that danged mat inside the door"

Gerry laughed hearty "I did warn you it's the one thing she can be funny about".

"Ach I'll keep an eye on myself", said Danny.

CHAPTER 20

He was glad to return to work and meet up with all the characters again. Most of the discussion in the canteen was about the happenings over the Christmas break. One of the more hardened drinkers try to out boast each other about how much they had to drink.

Terry announced one day he would be going back home permanently at Easter.

"Do you know what the idiot done when he was back there?" said Noel. "He went and fell in love and now he reckons he can't live without her".

The weeks rolled on and he continued the routine he had, Noel and Terry were now encouraging him to do more of the intricate work.

"You see, Noel explained. I need somebody to replace this boyo when he goes".

With the boys giving him advice Danny could feel himself getting better at the job.

A few days before the end of February when he arrived from work a message from home had arrived telling him to phone Duffins right away. His heart was pounding as he made the phone call. He knew something was seriously wrong. Maggie Duffin answered the phone and told him the sad news. Granny has taken a turn at ten O'clock and passed away just after twelve. He asked Maggie to let his parents know he would be home as quickly as he could. He sat for a long time at the foot of the stairs. He thought of all the arguments she and himself had. Sometime serious but mostly he was only taking a rise out of her. Gerry came in from work and he told him.

"Sorry to hear that, he said. I'm sure you'll go home".

"No doubt, answered Danny. I'm still stunned, I might get you to give me some advice how to get home".

"I'll do as much as I can to help Danny, Gerry replied.

"Do you know, the last thing she said to me. "Danny, I will never see you again, then she gave me these" Danny pulls the rosary beads from his pocket "These were her favourite rosary beads, she gave to me and told me to keep them in my pocket all the time and so I have".

Danny found the tears trickling down his cheeks "Danny I never see you again she said".

They both went in and told the landlady.

"Unfortunately Danny your grandparents are usually the first relatives to die in your lifetime", she said. "But she was a good age and what you've said it seems as though she was prepared to go".

Gerry and Danny sat down and lined out the trip home from trains to the boat to the bus that would deliver him to the village. Later that night his mother rang and he was able to tell her what time to expect him. All went as planned.

Train to the boat, to the bus and he took James McAnulla's taxi home. Even though it was a sad occasion he was looking forward to seeing all the folks at home. He thought about Jip the dog.

"I wonder how will he react to me, probably will still remember me".

His mother rushed out as soon as she saw the car and threw her arms around her weeping. They held each other both weeping for what seemed like ages.

"Come in" his mother said, and see your old sparring partner". He met his father coming down from the room "Welcome home Danny", he said as he shook his hand.

"She said she'd probably never see you again".

"Aye", said Danny. "She told me the same". There was just a neighbour couple in the room as he kneeled down beside the coffin and prayed, she looked so calm.

Pains had wrecked her life for so long "No more pains Granny", he whispered. His mother standing beside him repeated "No more pains".

One of the women that was giving a hand gave him tea and sandwiches. He just had them finished when he remembered about Jip.

"I'm looking forward to see how Jip reacts when he sees me", he said to his mother.

"Oh! I suppose you left England before my last letter arrived, said his mother. "In it I told you poor old Jip was found dead in the shed on Sunday week". "Ach no", answered Danny. "I was really looking forward to seeing him again" "You remember Danny he always lay in the hay shed at night", said Tess. "But a few nights after you left he moved to the turf shed and lay beside Pat Burkes bike. That's where your father found him. Poor Jip went through some manouvers the first month or so after you left". "He went up to the crossroads every day and Bosco was telling us he kept chasing that hare until the very end. I supposed he reckoned if you were about you would come some time for the bike".

All evening and night neighbours called, a constant stream coming and going. Sometime during the night he remarked to his mother.

"This woman must have been popular in her day, there's so many visitors".

"It's because of the wakes your da and Edmund Coyle attends", mother answered. Some asked him about life in London. Others hinted he might stay at home but he always said he had to go back but in a few months time he would probably come home for the summer. The Carlins, Martin's mother and father arrived, they apologised Martin couldn't attend as his back was "at him". Bosco called late on. Danny was sure he'd have a lot of questions to answer about London, his job and so on, but instead Bosco had a large problem of his own. He and his girlfriend Susan had fallen out a few nights before. He went into great detail about the row and was deeply upset. Danny excused himself every so often and went to talk to a recently arrived neighbours.

Bosco came over to him, "I'm going now Danny. I think I cycle in by the town and maybe come across Susan".

"Your in a bad way Bosco" said Danny, "I am sure you and Susan can sort your relationship out".

"Ach! Danny I hope so", said Bosco. "If we don't I'll go crazy".

"I'll be staying about for a few days after the funeral so we'll have a good long chat", Danny assured Bosco.

The next day, the day of the funeral was very hectic and Danny was glad to see the end of it. Eventually all the neighbours who had called back to the house left and he was alone with his parents for the first time since he arrived home.

"Tonight will be her first night away from this house in sixty four years" said his father. "Many times I heard her boast about it, sixty four years, a long time".

"I suppose it wasn't all sunshine", his mother replied. "Of course not, her first was born premature and died within hours, after she fell off the ladder searching for eggs in the hay shed", his father answered. "Then wee Mary was just three when she wandered down to the river and drowned. She blamed herself for both their deaths. I was less than a year old when my father died. He was just thirty four". Danny was shocked.

"I didn't know about your brother and sister, that must have been heart breaking". His father stared a long time into the fire before answering.

"The sad fact was she never spoke about any of them, that's why you never heard it. It was her way of dealing with it, I suppose it was just too painful to talk about it. It was probably the reason she was so religious. Anytime I would ask her about my father she always said he was a fine man who never got over the death of his daughter Mary. Then she would rush outside to do something".

That night in bed Danny went over and over all his father had told him and regretted not querying Granny more about her life.

The next morning Danny decided to leave the milk can down the road like old times. He headed up by the cross, he was about to listen for Jip racing the hare when it hit him that Jip was no more. A feeling of regret filled him, regret at not being there for Granny and Jip in their last days.

"Feck it anyway", he whispered to himself. "Both of them gone makes a big change".

Bosco had seen him coming and timed it perfectly to be at the crossroads the same time as Danny.

"A bit like old times", Bosco commented.

"Aye, Danny replied. "But our old warrior has gone to the dogs kennel in the sky".

"Well he raced that danged hare until the very end", said Bosco, and you know something I haven't seen her about since".

"Well have you and Susan sorted out your love life", asked Danny.

Bosco clapped his hands. "All is back to normal, I bumped into her the other night and even though she was frosty at first she came around in no time, I think it's made her more keener than ever".

"That's good man, I'd advise you to marry the girl, it's the first thing that'll settle you down", advised Danny. "She has hinted we should get engaged but I haven't two pence to rub together, how could I buy a dear engagement ring".

"Cassie Byrne will supply you with one out of her catalogue", laughed Danny.

"I already owe her money for a watch I got for Susan at Christmas. It won't be paid off until August".

"Hi! What about you, what's London like"?

"Well it's all going well at the minute", answered Danny. "I've good digs a good job and plenty of money".

Bosco kept asking him questions, how hard is the work? What does he do at night and at the weekends? Did he get to play any football? Danny answered all the questions hoping Bosco wouldn't twig on that he still hadn't settled down completely. They decided they'd meet again later on. As he travelled home Danny's head was muddled. In London he thought over here life would be simpler and sweeter but now he wasn't too sure, maybe life could be too dull . He knew his parents would be willing him to stay at home but he still would need to earn some more money before he could comeback. As the week went on he started to miss the buzz of London. He missed the craic in the canteen at work every day. He enjoyed clearing up one job and moving on to a new site, meeting a new set of characters. He also missed the Irish club at the weekends. There was something of a freedom about being away. If you want to go to see a film there was any amount of cinemas. A five minutes walk brought him to a subway station and the trains would leave you anywhere you'd want to go.

"Would you not think of staying? His mother asked him when he told her he was heading back on Saturday to be ready for work on Monday morning. He explained he'd go back for another few months and try and send as much home to install electricity and the phone.

"I like to think I'd have a car if I came back here", said Danny.

"IF", his mother said.

"All right", answered Danny. "When I come back".

Danny arrived back in London on the Sunday Morning, it was much easier leaving home than the last time. He assured his mother and father he'd return in a few months. Terry and Noel started a new contract on the first Monday back. It was a fairly large job and Noel reckoned it would take them up to Easter to complete it.

"Then that's the end of me here", said Noel. "I'm getting married on Easter Monday and were moving back to Wexford". Danny was surprised "What will Terry do for a partner"? he asked.

"Ach! there's a young boyo he knows called Danny Higgins might give him a hand out", said Noel.

"Your codding", answered Danny.

"Why not", replied Noel. "You've been helping us out at times and you will be able to handle it alright, you are well capable, keep a close eye on what we're doing for the next couple of months and you'll be fine".

Danny thought this would be a great feather in his cap and took a great interest in how the two boys went about things from then on.

CHAPTER 21

One night at the club one of the regulars Nancy OFee introduced him to her younger sister Nora, just over from Clare. Danny and her seemed to hit it off right away. As the night progressed it was evident she liked Danny. Danny hinted he could walk her and Nancy home.

"As long as you're not expecting a large meal", Nora joked.

Danny and Nora become an item. Every Saturday they met up at the club and on Wednesday nights they'd would usually go to the cinema. Some Saturdays they would go to watch Spurs play or go sightseeing or just walk around the shops. They were very comfortable in each other's company. On Sundays Danny usually went for his walk around the park. After an half an hour or so he'd come back and sit on a bench near the entrance to the park. One Sunday he was sitting watching some young lads playing football. Families made up of parents and offspring would saunter by. Couples and individuals some walking dogs passed by. One Sunday Danny heard a high pitched voice causing great commotion. As this person got closer it turned out to be a girl shouting out a name. Before Danny realised what was happening a dog with a lead still attached to it came bounding his way and started jumping up on him. Then he heard the girl shouting to keep hold of the dog so he grabbed the lead and then a black girl arrived. She thanked Danny profusely and scolded Cindy the dog for breaking away. The girl well and truly out of breath, sat down on the bench beside Danny. This was the first time Danny realised he had a conversation with a black person. He was a bit hesitant at the start but this girl was so open and friendly he was very comfortable in her company. They spoke about the dog, its breed how old it was so on. She introduced herself as Jennifer. They made small talk for five minutes or so. Then she announced to Danny she would keep Cindy on the move. As she rose from the seat she shook Danny's hand and thanked him again for catching her dog. When she left Danny thought what a pleasant girl she was.

During the week Danny didn't think any more of Jennifer. The following Sunday he repeated his usual routine walking around the park and ending up sitting on the same bench near the park entrance. It was only then Jennifer came into his mind, but almost immediately his thoughts were disrupted by the sight of Jennifer with Cindy in tow coming bouncing along the path. He wondered would she recognise him.

As she came near she waved "Hello Danny, I've kept a tight hold on Cindy today". She sat down produced a packet of peppermint sweets and told Danny to take a few. The conservation continued as from the week before. She told Danny she lived not far from the other side of the park. She also explained she was attending college and told him the make up of her family and the name of her boyfriend. She enquired of Danny what his situation was and seemed very interested in what he told her. Danny felt very comfortable with her and when she left he felt a bit sad. During the week he thought more about Jennifer than before, not in a romantic way. She had told him all about her boyfriend. It was in a more of a friendship way. The next Sunday an exact repeat of what happened the Sunday before. "We'll have to stop meeting like this", joked Jennifer as she sat down.

Again the conversation moved along smoothly. She told Danny what she hoped to make of her life and coaxed Danny to line out what his dreams were, during the conversation Danny spied from the corner of his eye his landlady and her companion coming through the park gate. They started to come down the path towards them but when she was about fifty yards away she spied Danny and Jennifer stopped then turned and walked the opposite way. Jennifer didn't see their action but Danny thought right away the landlady would probably comment on it later on and so it turned out.

When he arrived back that evening he could sense the atmosphere was frosty. During tea Mrs Murray asked him was the girl he was talking to black. Danny explained how a few weeks before her dog had broken away and came over to where he was sitting.

"When Jennifer, its owner arrived she sat down and thanked me", said Danny. "Now every Sunday since we do have a wee conservation".

"Well", said Mrs Murray, "it's no business of mine but you should be weary of her type". Danny could feel his temper rising.

"What type do you think she is Mrs Murray"? asked Danny.

"All I'm saying is those ones are worth keeping an eye on".

"She seems a very nice girl as far as I'm concerned", answered Danny.

"With you being only here a short time I'm just saying a lot of her kind can't be trusted", said Mrs Murray.

Danny didn't answer for a while. This could cause a rift between them and for the moment that wouldn't suit Danny.

"Well anyway", he said, "if she comes over and sits beside me on a park bench I can't really stop her". Before she could answer Danny rose and disappeared up to his bedroom. Later on when Gerry came to his room, he knocked on his door and entered. He told him the whole story. Gerry had a good laugh.

"I wouldn't pass much remarks on her, I suppose she'd say she doing it for your own good but, I always take people no matter what their colour, religion, politics or where they have come from, as I find them myself and not what somebody else thinks about them. In the building trade you'll hear the Irish Paddies running down the English, Welsh or Scots. When they're sick of that they usually start running down fellas from Ireland because they come from a different county than themselves".

They talked for another while and when Danny was leaving Gerry giggled.

"I still think if you landed back in Ireland with her it would be the talk of the country for a while.

"Maybe", replied Danny. But I think she'd get a better reception there than if I landed back here some night with her".

Every Sunday Danny sat on the same bench and around about the same time, Jennifer and Cindy come bounding down the path. Even the dog got to know Danny and came over tail wagging. Jennifer came and sat down. She had always a piece of news to tell Danny. Sometimes it was of no real interest to Danny but he always made his view known especially if Jennifer was seeking advice. Most of the time it was about her studies at college, other times it was something concerning mates of hers. She always had sweets or chocolate she'd share with Danny. About the tenth Sunday the routine continued as before but Danny realised that Jennifer was more subdued than before. Danny enquired was everything alright.

She shrugged her shoulders, "I'm having a spot of boyfriend trouble". Danny tried to get her to elaborate. But she didn't.

"Thanks Danny for listening to my moaning, I promise I'll be happier next Sunday".

As she left she shouted back, "see you then".

Danny watched as she went out of sight. He was about to go for another stroll when out of the blue two burly men clamped themselves down one each side of Danny. He attempted to rise but one of them pushed him down.

"We've been watching you for some time sir", said the biggest of the two.

"What do you mean?" asked Danny "We have a few questions to ask you", the stranger continued.

"What about"? enquired Danny. He took a long drag of his cigarette then the stranger asked, "How well do you know that girl?"

"Jennifer", said Danny. "I know very little about her, she comes over and sits down here most Sundays".

"Every Sunday for quite a while", said the smaller one, "and she gives you something every day, what is it?"

Danny could feel himself filling up with fear "sweets or chocolate", answered Danny.

"What real interest have you in her"? the big one queried.

Danny let a nervous giggle. "I have no interest in her, why should I she has a boyfriend".

Oh! so you know her boyfriend", the smaller one said.

"No I don't know her boyfriend but she mentioned a few Sundays ago she had a boyfriend", Danny replied. "So you meet this girl every Sunday, she gives you sweets or something", said the big one but you know nothing about her".

"Why should I know anything about her", announced Danny. "I don't go looking for her, her dog broke away from her one Sunday and I happened to catch it, from then on she comes over and sits for a few minutes and then leaves".

"After she gives you sweets or something", said the smaller one. The bigger one buts in "what do you think of these sweets?" "I eat them", Danny answered. "Look I don't know what you want from me but I don't have anything else to tell you. I'm only came over from Ireland a few months ago, I'm living up near the top of the road in digs and I come for a walk here every Sunday, that's it. Do you know I don't even know that girls surname". "Mavarro" the big one replied. They both rose and confabbed for a while. "What's your surname"? asked the big one. "Higgins", answered Danny.

He pulled out a notebook and as he wrote he said slowly "Danny Higgins".

At that they were gone as quickly as they came. Danny didn't move for a while in case they might be watching and make out he was very nervous, then it struck him.

"How did they know his Christian name was Danny, he hadn't mention it". "What in jayus was that all about", he thought.

He got up, left the park and walked down a few side streets. Every now and then he'd look behind him to see if anybody was following him.

That evening he confided in Gerry "Strange", said Gerry, "they must be cops. That's the worst thing about this place you don't know who you're talking to. Something that seems so innocent could turn into a problem". "The first week I was here I was walking along the footpath when this woman seemed to trip and fall in front of me, I gave her a hand up and asked was she alright. Another younger girl came over and thanked me for being kind to her mother. It was only about an hour later when I went to buy something I found they'd stolen my wallet. Dangerous talking to any strangers".

"Well I'll be staying far away from that park on Sundays from now on", said Danny.

"Aye right you'd be", said Gerry. "She might be friendly enough but maybe someone else is using her to set you up".

That night he mentioned what had happened to Nora O'Fee, she asked a lot of questions about how he met this girl.

When Danny completed his story, Nora shook her head "Watch yourself Danny, this place isn't like home. Keep yourself to yourself, you just don't know what agenda some of these people have". Danny decided not to elaborate any more on Jennifer even though he was convinced she was just a nice friendly girl. Now and then at work he found himself thinking back on the whole episode which had taken place on Sunday. On Tuesday after dinner he made his way to the corner shop. On these shopping trips he always brought something home to Mrs Murray, maybe ham, fruit or a cake.

"Ach Danny your too decent", she'd say. "I don't expect anything".

He was looking around to see what he could take back with him, when spied the local evening paper. What he saw on the front page made him gasp. A fairly large photograph of a smiling Jennifer and above it in large letters was the word MURDERED. He was so stunned. He bought the paper and didn't delay until he reached his bedroom. He started reading, Jennifer Marvarro the nineteen year old daughter of a prominent business man Zach Marvarro was found dead in a dark alleyway, not far from her home last night. Her parents are devastated.

Her mother said "She was the joy of our life, very seldom you would find her without a smile on her face".

The report explained the couple had another daughter and a son. It ended up saying a twenty one year old man was in custody. Danny read it a few times. He just couldn't understand how anyone could kill such a lovely human being. Again he waited until he heard Gerry arrive up to his room, he showed him the paper.

"I just can't get over it", Danny said. "I had taken a funny kind of liking for her, we just seemed to click, we discussed a lot of things. All that fuss on Sunday must have been part of it".

Gerry agreed. "Didn't she tell you she had boyfriend bother. There's a good chance he done it".

That night Danny found himself wondering should he try and contact her family and tell them what she had told him but in the end he decided to keep mute.

"What good would it do", he thought only maybe get himself into further trouble".

Danny kept an eye on the paper every evening, later on it the week an article confirmed that her boyfriend was charged with her murder. The following Sunday Danny didn't go to the park, he walked in the opposite direction. After a while he came on a beautiful riverside walk. "This will have to do he thought".

Every month Danny sent money home, his mother insisted he keep it for himself as they were financially sound. But he explained this money was for the improvements he'd need when he eventually returned for good. Terry left a few weeks before Easter and Noel followed to act as best man for him. Noel returned and now the two of them carried on working together. Noel insisted all monies would be halved equally and this left Danny now earning more. As summer approached Danny remarked to Noel he had promised his father he'd return home and help him to harvest the crops.

"That suits me fine, said Noel. I can go home for a week or so, then I'll come back and work at the house I bought last year, it needs a lot of repairs. You can return when you want too". Danny stayed at home for five weeks, at first he enjoyed the fine treatment he received everywhere he went. Everybody wanted to know what his life was like in London and was curious to find out if he was staying at home. After a few weeks he was looking forward to returning to London. Again he was puzzled for when in London he yearned for home and now he wasn't sure if his life back in Ireland would satisfy him. In the end he came to the conclusion if he continued to work in London and go home for four or five weeks in the summer, maybe a shorter visit at Christmas it would leave everyone happy and he would have the best of both worlds.

CHAPTER 22

WHAT EVER HAPPENED TO THE DREAM

"Come on, it's time to rise and shine", shouted Rusty.

Danny moved in the bed "Jaysus", he said to himself. "This bloody hand must be broken". The more limbs he moved the more pain he inflicked.

Rusty came into the bedroom "How are you feeling?" he asked Danny.

"Bloody awful", was the reply "What about you?"

Rusty done a quick examination of himself "Ach I'm not too bad considering there was four of them, they could have killed us".

I don't remember much about it", said Danny "or how did it start?".

Rusty took a slug from the whiskey bottle he was holding. "The usual, drink", he answered. "Drink an argument and then all hell was let loose. Of course they thought as there was four of them they'd take us no bother but they found out to their cost you shouldn't mess with Higgins or Big Rusty."

Danny gingerly eased himself out of bed. "I'm not sure where we won or not, I'm aching all over".

Rusty let a laugh "Oh! we won ok, those boys had to hoof it. Here take a drop of that", he handed Danny a whiskey bottle and he drained what was left in it.

Rusty looked at his watch "Right", he said. "The train leaves in an hour and a half so we need to be making tracks, by the time we have a few swallows and then hit the station our time will be limited".

They were leaving London for a visit to Rustys brother Hamish's place in Kinochlevin, Scotland, Rusty was a large man over six feet in height. He had a head of curly orange hair and an orange beard hence the nick name Rusty. Danny and Rusty worked together for the last four years. They were classed as the best at their trade of paving. Some contractors wouldn't use any others. When they started a job they worked seven days a week until it was finished then they went on a binge that could last until their money was gone and then they'd go back and start another job.

When they were drinking, anything could happen. Both of them were rushed several times to casualty after being involved in a fight. This would be their third trip to Hamish's place. He farmed a small holding up in the Highlands. Hamish was the exact image of Rusty, the only difference, he lived on his wits. He spent much of his time fishing for salmon, illegally. He also brewed his own alcohol away out in the hills therefore was always in trouble with the authorities.

As they boarded the train Rusty commented "I hope this Hamish man has been busy this last few weeks for I feel a terrible drouth coming on.".

"We'll bring a supply with us just in case", announced Danny. "How long will it take us Rusty"?

"We'll have three trains to catch, so I would be pleased enough if we were up there by ten o'clock tonight".

Armed with a bottle of whiskey each they settled in for a long trip. Before the train pulled out Danny noticed a young lad of around eighteen carrying a suitcase covered with Irish tricolour stickers. He was reading from a piece of paper and seemed unsure where he was going.

"Another recruit from Ireland", he remarked to Rusty.

"That was me twenty two years ago", Rusty laughed. "Ach you weren't as green as that guy"

"Indeed I was and probably more so", answered Danny.

He took a slug from the bottle, muttered to himself "Be a good lad turn and go home, there's nothing here for you, nothing. Back home to your parents, your friends and kindly neighbours. Walk down the quiet country roads, linger by the tiny streams, listen to the wildbirds, you probably were told this was the land of opportunities. A place to make your fortune. No, take my advice and go home, it was all lies".

As the train pulled away, the young lad was still standing reading his note.

"Aye, twenty two years and around this time of the year, wasted years".

Rusty took another mouthful from his bottle, settled down and seemed to doze off.

Danny couldn't erase the young lad out of his head. He still remembered clearly that fine August day Gerry O'Grady lifted him. His father wasn't there, it would have been too hard to bear, his granny telling him he wouldn't see her alive again. She was right. Jips tail wagging, his innocent eyes staring up at him. He wouldn't see him alive again either. He remembered seeing his mother standing at the hole in the hedge following the progress of the car up the hill until is disappeared out of sight. He recalled all the noise and fumes of the London traffic. His first day at work standing outside the Red Lion waiting to be collected. The awlful commotion of men arguing and fighting, some drunk from the weekend, others with cuts and black eyes. After twenty minutes he'd made up his mind, he wasn't staying but he did stay. The first ten years were fine. He picked up the trade of paving fairly quickly. Terry and Noel Mangan were very good to him in that respect. Then there was Mrs Murray, the landlady, so kind, so caring. She chastised him for coming in drunk a few nights and wasn't happy when she saw him speaking to a black girl in the park.

"Stay away from her kind", she warned him. "Their lifestyle is different from ours".

Gerry O'Grady moved to Liverpool where his girlfriend was nursing. A few months after Danny left and rented a bedsit.

Terry and Noel both went back to Ireland in the one year, Terry got married in April and Noel left the following Christmas. Danny struck up a working relationship with a Sligo lad, now seeing as he was the boss he was making even more money. He'd bought Terry and Noels tools and he purchased a small van. Every year he went back home for a month or so, in time to help save the crops. He made sure his parents wanted for nothing. He had the phone and electricity installed. He purchased a cheap tractor and instructed Bosco to teach his father to drive, so it would be easier than walking through the fields. He contracted Barney Farley to build on a bathroom and do other repairs to the house. One year his father announced to him he'd received the pension and was intending to cut back on the farming. Every year they enquired if he'd any notion of staying home permanently and each year he promised he'd think about it.

Bosco and Susan married in that time and owing to his father's health, he had a stroke, Bosco was now running the farm.

"That was what all the shouting at me done to him", Bosco joked.

In those first ten years Danny had quite a few girlfriends but none he felt could settle down with. He was always popular up at the club. He became a member of the pool and darts team. He never drank much more than 3 pints a night. Every so often he would go for a quiet drink in The Spinning Wheel bar. One night, it was his twenty seventh birthday, he decided to have a drink there for he hadn't visited it for quite a while. The new barmaid was gorgeous and Danny fell for her right away. Anouskia from Sweden. Anouskia felt the same about Danny. Three years of bliss followed. They were madly in love and so so happy. Danny took out his hankie and wiped a tear from his eye. Seven years later and he still found it hard to think about her. They were making plans to marry and settle down, so they'd spent a weekend house hunting. They decided on a one they both thought was ideal. Anouskia took a half day off to visit the estate agent, sign the documents and pay the deposit. Danny held his head in his hands. He had been through this torture a thousand times, Why! Why he thought. It doesn't get any easier. Millions upon millions of people in London, why should it have to be Anouskia who was in the wrong place at the wrong time. Word spread quickly through the site where he was working that a car bomb had exploded and there was casualities. He remembered thinking there would be traffic disruption, he had hoped to have made it home early to find out if Anouskia had been to the estate agent. Danny took another few mouthfuls of whiskey.

Witnesses say the passengers door hit her full on sending her fifty yards down the street, seven killed including the driver of the car. He still feels sick when he thinks about it. Where would his life have been now if Anouskia hadn't been killed?

"Ach! Christ", he said out loud, it wakened Rusty.

"What's wrong with you", he asked Danny. "My bloody head is fierce sore", he lied.

"Well you should stop belting men with it", joked Rusty. "Someday you'll hit the wrong guy"

"Jaysus do you hear him", Danny replied. "Wasn't it you once again who started that handling last night".

Rusty let a giggle, "Me, not likely sure I'm a big civil Scotsman".

"Aye and I'm wee Irish Leprechaun", answered Danny. Hamish met them at the train station in his rickle of a van. They stopped off and stocked up with booze. It would be all needed in the days ahead. They had just finished a large job. They'd worked sixteen days without a break. Now it was recreation time. Hamish had stocked up in fish, meat and his homemade hooch.

Most days were nothing but a haze, some nights they'd visit the nearest pub and most nights Rusty would end up in a dispute with someone. The owner would usually ease them outside and then lock up. A few bars around the area wouldn't serve them at all, having been involved in fights in former years. Then one day Rusty appeared with an oven ready hen. "Where did you come upon that?" asked Hamish.

Rusty replied. "It's one of yours that I captured in the yard".

Hamish rushed out, a minute later he appeared, "you rotten ugly cur", shouted Hamish. "You killed my favourite hen, Daisy, I'll split you open you good for nothing bastard".

"Did you expect us to die with hunger", said Rusty. "There's no food in the house".

Hamish swung a punch at him and hit him firmly on the mouth. Blood poured from it right away, Rusty rushed at Hamish and they both fell to the floor flaying away at each other. Danny tried to intervene but with his head blighted by the booze when he stooped down he could see two of each, Rusty and Hamish. He gave up and went over and sat down watching these two giants trying to get the better of each other. After what seemed like hours and both exhausted they finally got to their feet. Rusty's right eye was almost closed, blood pouring from a nasty gash on Hamish's eyebrow.

"Clear off and don't set your foot in this place again", said Hamish. "Killing my wee daisy"

"Not unless I want to die with hunger", Rusty replied.

"You lousy hoor", sobbed Hamish. "You know full well there is any amount of salmon in the blue barrel in the bedroom".

"I'm sick of eating fish", said Rusty. "I needed some variety". Hamish, now trying to stem the blood flowing all over his face "Well you won't ever have that problem here again".

"It was only a bloody hen", said Rusty.

"It wasn't any hen it was my wee Daisy", Hamish answered. Danny rose and went outside, he reckoned it could all start up again. He walked down the back lane that led him into a small tree surrounded field. A civil cow rushed over towards him. He scratched its neck and the cow licked his coat.

"How did life take such a downturn"? he thought.

When Anouskia was killed he lost the will to live. The whole energy drained from his body. He couldn't concentrate, depression set it. Day or night he might forget about Anouskia for a minute or so, then it would hit him again and that was the worst of all. He thought of going home and telling his parents about what had happened to the beautiful girl he planned to share his life with. The sweetheart who had made him so blissfully happy, now gone, the laughter, her gorgeous smile and all the love they shared. He decided against it. Instead he visited all the haunts where Anouskia and he used to frequent, maybe, just maybe it was all a bad dream. He called in to the Spinning Wheel bar and sat in their favourite seat beside the open fire but it only hurt more. He trudged along the paths they walked frequently, nothing helped.

Danny sauntered up the field followed by the friendly cow, standing on the headridge he could see the valley below, a small stream trickled along. It reminded him of the back fields on Pat Burkes farm where Emma, Pats niece and himself spent time walking and talking. He smiled when he thought of those days. He genuinely felt he was in love with

Emma, but now he knew it was only a fleeting fancy so far from the feeling he enjoyed with Anouskia.

"I better go back", he said to himself. "God knows what I'll find up there, one dead body, maybe two".

He headed towards the house and gingerly moved towards the door, silence, then an enormous burst of laughter filled the air.

When Hamish saw him he let a roar, "Come in Danny and get a fill up".

"I wasn't sure what I might find said Danny, two corpses that I'd have to bury". Rusty, now with his eye almost closed claimed "It's all sorted Danny, "I promised to pay compensation for the deceased bird, it's now being cooked, all's well that ends well".

CHAPTER 23

Two days later they decided to travel home again. Before they left London they were offered a large job which was to be ready soon. Armed with the compulsory bottle of whiskey each, they caught the train to Glasgow. They had an hour or so to wait until they caught the next train. Danny remembered it was Sunday the designated day to phone home, no matter what he was doing or what shape he was in he always managed to phone home. Sometimes it was a brief call, other times he would find out all the news around home and make his mother feel he was interested in it. He found a call box in a quiet corner, he was surprised when it was answered by Bosco, it struck him something was wrong, and so there was. Bosco conveyed the bad news, his father had taken a bad turn a few days before and his health deteriorated since. The doctor gave him hours to live.

"Put mammy on Bosco," said Danny.

He knew she was in a bad way.

"How soon can you get home Danny"? she asked.

"I feared he wouldn't last to Sunday so I could tell you".

"I'm in Glasgow now so I'll take the train down to the boat and I'll be home early tomorrow".

"I hope to God he'll hold on to I make it home. I'll phone you before I get on the boat".

"Please do", answered his mother. "Father McManus gave him the last rights a couple of hours ago". He went back to the bar where Rusty was and told him the sad news.

"You may travel to London on your own, for I promised my mother I'll be home as soon as I can, so I'll take the train down to the boat".

"Ach! no", said Rusty. "I can't let you make that lonesome journey on your own".

Danny examined Rusty's face, his eye was completely black, there was still caked blood on parts of his face and his clothes looked as though he rolled about the floor in them, which he had done.

"I'll be grand", insisted Danny. "You make your way home and secure a bit of work for us".

"I'll do no such thing", Rusty replied. "We'll travel over together, you need a bit of company on that journey, anyway I never been to Ireland and I've always heard the wakes over there are mighty binges altogether".

A few hours later they were at the docks, Danny found a phone and phoned home, Bosco answered again.

The news wasn't good, "he passed away just over an hour ago", he said.

Danny didn't particular want to talk to his mother. "It's hard to console someone over the phone", he thought.

"Tell mum I'll be home about midday tomorrow", he said.

They travelled overnight and got a couple of buses to the village. They had spent most of the night at the bar. Danny answered all the questions Rusty want to know about his father.

"A quiet civil man", he said. "He didn't spend too many nights away from home. Always content when he was out among the animals or working in the fields. I can say without fear of contradiction I never saw him lose his temper".

As they disembarked from the bus Rusty suggested they have another whiskey or so before they'd get a taxi out to the house.

"You can have one if you want but I won't bother", said Danny.

There were four fellows in the bar. Rusty went up and ordered two double whiskeys and brought them down to the snug where Danny was sitting. He handed Danny one of the glasses.

"Here throw that into you, you have a ardious few hours to come", he said. They drank the whiskeys. "I'm getting another one for myself", said Rusty.

"Well just one more, the poor man will be buried before we make it home", answered Danny. As Rusty headed up to the bar the men and barman were in deep conversation. Rusty heard one of the men saying "Dan Higgins was a civil man, he never done anyone a bad turn". Another one asked the barman "Where did the good for nothing son go"?

"Ach he's somewhere in England", answered the bar man.

"Not much odds where he is", said another man. "I hear them say the mother mightn't hear from him from one year to the next".

Rusty ordered his drink just as another one commented, "no good lousy hoor". Rusty swung around with his fist and caught him full on the nose. Danny heard the commotion and when he looked up he saw them all raining punches on Rusty. Swiftly he joined in the malee. Danny and Rusty had been in many predicaments like this before. They always planned to position themselves back to back so no one could hit them from behind. After a short time Danny felt they were getting on top of the situation, suddenly the barman appeared with a couple of hurley sticks, he gave one to each of the men and all started to batter Danny and Rusty. Danny realised they were not only outnumbered but now they had weapons.

Blood was pouring from several cuts on Rusty's face and he himself had received several mighty blows to the head.

"Run for it", he yelled. The both of them rushed out through the door followed by the assailants.

"Don't come back", roared the barman. "There's more where that came from".

As they rushed down the street Danny heard one of them say, "Who the Christ are they"? They went up around the corner and sat down on a stone wall.

"Only the barman produced those bats we would have taken them", Rusty announced.

Danny examined Rusty's face, there was blood everywhere with his unruly red hair and a large beard now soaked with blood he would have frightened the devil. Danny's head was splitting, he felt it and come upon bump after bump, blood was also pouring down his face from where he couldn't say.

"We can't go back to the house like this", he thought.

Then he came up with the idea of going to James McAnulla, he was the taxi man, now retired. If his mother or father was needing to take a car to go somewhere James even though retired would still bring them. Anytime he was going home or away James always obliged.

"Come on", he said to Rusty. "We'll get ourselves cleaned up before we head out home".

James was shocked when he saw them but he brought them in and showed them where the bathroom was. Danny just told James they had a mishap but didn't elaborate. With sticking plasters supplied by James they eventually curtailed the bleeding. Rustys black eye from the fight with Hamish stood out amongst the red hair and blood.

Bosco and a few other men were at the door when they pulled on to the street.

Danny got out and went over and hugged Bosco.

"I'm glad for your mother's sake you made it", he said. Then he stepped back, "good lord, what the devil happened you"?

"Ach we had a bit of a mishap", answered Danny.

Rusty had now ascended from the car and came towards the men.

"This is Rusty McKenzie he was a recipient of the same mishap.

"Push in", Bosco said. "Your mother will be pleased to see you" glad to have them replaced elsewhere.

His mother came in from the room and threw her arms around him and clung to him, crying loudly. Rusty hung about outside. Eventually Danny and his mother made their way to where his father's remains lay. Anybody who was in the bedroom made their way to the sitting room and left the two of them alone.

"Did he suffer mum", asked Danny.

"No, or if he did he didn't say", explained Tess. "But he raving a lot this last few days, no sense in what he was saying, sometimes he'd be looking for you to do something. Other times he'd want Edmund Coyle to ask him something. Of course poor Edmund is dead four years now but he didn't seem to have any pain". They knelt down and prayed at the bedside. Danny couldn't help feeling bad, not being about in his father's last years. He cried like a baby, was it worth it, what he'd done? Danny had to explain to his mother that he and his pal who had travelled with him had an unfortunate mishap. He went to the door and signalled to Rusty to come in.

"This is Rusty McKenzie mum", he said. "Rusty, this is my mother".

His mother blurted out a hello and Danny could see her recoiling.

"My god", she said. "You must be in awful pain".

"Nothing a wee drop of the hard stuff wouldn't cure Mrs Higgins", Rusty announced.

"Well you might get a drop of tea", said Tess. "But the hard staff could be difficult enough to come by in this house".

All through the evening and night Danny met and greeted quite a few of the neighbours, some of the younger ones wouldn't really have remembered him. Rusty prowled about unable to settle. Every now and then he'd ask Danny when would the booze appear. Danny lead him on for a while but in the end he had to tell him, with his mother being a pioneer there would be no alcohol in the house.

"What in Christ is a pioneer?" he asked.

"A teetotal", Danny explained. "My father might have a bottle of stout if he was in the fair or mart but no more than two.

"What the devil happened you"? said Rusty shaking his head.

"I don't know but I could near guarantee if I'd still have been living here I wouldn't have been a big drinker either", said Danny.

The next day was the day of the funeral. The priest in his homily pointed out how a civil honest man Dan was. "There isn't a neighbour or anyone who had any dealings with Dan Higgins didn't find him anything only a proper gentleman, now he is safely up in heaven receiving his just reward".

Some of the close neighbours and friends were invited back to the house for food.

Rusty approached Danny as they left the graveyard. "Have we to stay much longer before we travel back to London"? he queried.

"I might stay a few days", said Danny but if you want to head back sooner it'll be alright with me".

"Ok" answered Rusty. "I'll make my way back to the village and if I catch an early bus I might still get the boat tonight".

Danny asked Bosco would he run Rusty into the village, "Oh! and whatever you do don't go into O Hagans bar. There would be a good chance both of you could be killed".

Again Danny had long talks with neighbours. Sometimes he didn't tell them was the entire the truth. Owenie Carlin quizzed him about several aspects of his life. Danny told him he'd just purchased his third house. He had several vintage cars and now had a dozen men working for him.

"That's why I had to send Rusty back today", he explained. "To make sure things are running smoothly. As far as Danny was concerned Owenie seemed to believe all he had told him. Owenie mentioned Martin had just taken over the insurance firm he worked for. When everyone left that evening himself and his mother had a long chat.

"Who or what is that big monster with the red hair"? questioned his mother. "Or how did you become pals".

Danny told her about how they met. It was about a year after Anouskia was killed.

"I just couldn't get over her death", Danny sighed. "I was deeply depressed. Work a day or two in the week, enough to get by but I was slowly sinking deeper and deeper into oblivion, then I was working on a site, at this stage I was just casual labouring because it was all I was fit for when I happen to be talking to Rusty, he was laying paving bricks. I told him that was my trade. He said he was desperately looking for help and coaxed me to join him. It was the first time I could see the light at the end of the tunnel, we just clicked".

Danny explained to his mother how he poured his all woes out to Rusty. When he finished a hugh weight was lifted off his shoulders. Rusty also confided in Danny. He told him of his early life in Scotland, how he moved to Glasgow, met a girl and married but with having a short temper the relationship was volatile, then after a year they had a wee boy. His son was about three when one evening he came home and both son and wife were gone. Of course he and his wife had an awful row the night before. It was three years since he has saw his son

"As hard a man as he was", Danny said, "he sobbed and cried like a child".

Danny explained to his mother they were good for each other. They worked hard, long hours and makes good money.

"Of course we spend some", remarked Danny. Danny stayed at home a week and he thoroughly enjoyed his time with his mother. They talked long into the night about his father and Granny.

"Did he say much about me leaving"? asked Danny.

"Ach" now it was very sore on us all", answered Tess. "But we found our own wee way to cope. Then one night he told me that when he was around twenty he got a chance to go with someone to England but when he told his mother she was so annoyed he scrapped the idea. I think it made him understand better your reason for going. He said he would never have stopped you from going for he still remembered how disappointed he was".

Every day he borrowed Bosco's car and both of them visited Dan's grave, then in the evening they'd stroll through the fields.

"This was your fathers favourite place on the farm", his mother said as they climbed up to the highest field. "He always said he saw so many of the neighbours farms from here, there was always something interesting taking place. He told me one calm day he heard someone shouting quite a distance away, he decided to investigate. He travelled to where the shouting came from and found an old man called Harry Reilly pinned under a tree, he'd been cutting. After he rescued him he became a hero and was the talk of the country. Another summers morning just as the sun was rising, he was looking down on the valley when he spied a man walking at speed along the back of a hedge, your father stood in out of sight. He realised it was buck well known for stealing and he had a turf spade with him. That night when he ceildhed in some neighbours house, it's transpired they had a turf spade taken out of the bog. Your father waited until he got the thief away at Mass one Sunday, went and searched his sheds, found the turf spade and brought it back to the rightful owner".

The week passed quickly. The night before he was leaving his mother became very teary. Danny lined out to her what his intentions were. He planned to work another year, save as much as he could and come home for good.

"I'll have no bother finding work with contractors here in Ireland. Anyway the wages is not near as good as when I landed over there twenty two years ago".

Bosco left him into the bus and on way Danny repeated to him the plan he had revealed to his mother.

"Keep a wee eye on her like a good man", said Danny.

"I'm over every day anyway seeing I have the land taken", answered Bosco. "Me and her gets on like a house on fire and she always has sweets or money for our youngsters".

When he was alone on the boat he started to think about the different lifestyle Bosco has compared to him. Himself and Susan had three children, Bosco's father moved to live with one of the daughters because of his bad health and needed much more care so now Bosco was the farm owner. His mother was still pretty fresh woman and lived with Bosco and Susan. The children, he thought bonded all together, Bosco, his mother and Susan. His mind wandered and he couldn't help but wonder if Anouskia hadn't been killed and they had children how life could have been different, not for the first time a terrible sadness filled him.

"It's not too late", he thought. "I'll work hard, save all I can and go back home to mum in a year or so and start over again".

When he arrived back Rusty had just procured a fairly large job to start on Monday. That night he told Rusty of his plans. He explained he was going to work another year or so, drink less and save a bit and go back home to his mother. Before he'd finished his story he could see Rusty was itching to tell him something. It turned out Hamish had sent him a letter which had come from his wife. In the letter she revealed she was living in Edinburgh and their son was now twelve! And kept asking about his father. She suggested they meet sometime for the son's sake.

"I sat down and wrote back to her", said Rusty. "And told her I was willing to meet them anytime, I'm waiting on her to reply".

Danny could see that a chance to meet excited Rusty.

"Do you know Danny I'll do the same as you, save up a few pounds and if things work out we might make a go of it the second time around".

They talked long into the night about how they made a mess of their lives and both agreed it was time for change.

They stuck to their plan working long hours and cutting back on the booze. The contractors they were now working for was very happy with their work and had other jobs lined up for them before they'd have the last finished. As the weeks passed, Rusty had another letter from his wife, she pointed out they could meet some Sunday for a few hours but it would be sometime yet before it happened. Rusty wrote back and proposed she should take her time whatever plans she made he'd be happy to go along with. Since a mention about meeting Danny could see a vast improvement in Rusty's attitude. The next letter had a phone number for Rusty to ring. As he came off the phone he whopped with delight, they had arranged to meet at a service station. The meeting went well and the son, as well as Rusty was anxious to extend the affair.

Danny kept in touch much more with his mother, often phoning her several times a week. He also gave Bosco a call now and again to make sure she wasn't too lonely. A few months down the line Rusty made arrangements and travelled up to Edinburgh. Danny decided at the last minute he'd travel home for the weekend. Both trips went without a hitch. Danny's mother was delighted to see him and Rusty returned invigorated "More of the same was needed" he claimed.

CHAPTER 24

A FORK IN THE ROAD

Miss Kilfedder, senior Councillor in the alcoholic unit of the Blue Skies Addiction Centre wrote down a few notes.

Then she hinted to Danny, "All was going well with the both of you".

"Yes", Danny sighed, "very well".

He explained to Miss Kilfedder they had turned their lives around. They still drank a bit, but no wild binges like before. Rusty was now spending more time with Irene and James up in Edinburgh. Danny had purchased a van and travelled home to visit his mother every few months. He sailed over on Friday night spent Saturday and Sunday with her and arrived back in time for work on Monday morning. His mother was coping well. Bosco had rented the land and called every day. Bosco's mother and her travelled to bingo two nights a week. Both enjoyed the few days spent with each other.

Rusty mentioned often his desire to move back to Scotland but all at the moment was ideal and he didn't like to change anything in case it would fall apart.

"We couldn't have been happier", said Danny. "I met a girl in the Irish Centre and we enjoyed each other's company, she was very keen to further our relation, but platonic suited me just then, so it kinda faded out".

A prolonged silence filled the room.

"I know it's very hard to talk about the events that turned your life completely around", said Miss Kilfedder. "But maybe if you share them with me it just might ease your agony".

Danny shuffled uneasily on his chair and stared at the ceiling.

"Very very difficult", he muttered.

"Take your time", whispered Miss Kilfedder.

Eventually Danny began to tell the story of October the first. It was the same as any other day, they were working laying paving brick around a new catholic church in the north of the city. They had been there four weeks or more and was half way finished. They liked the job because they got on well with Canon OLeary, the priest in charge. They had christened him Cooper because they both agreed he looked much like Gary Cooper. They even told him and he took it in good spirits. They found out he had a dry sense of humour like themselves. Nearly every day they had good banter about converting Rusty to Catholicism.

"I'm a good Scottish Presbyterian", Rusty would remind them. "And that's the way I'm staying". One day a lorry load of paving brick arrived and Rusty showed the driver where he wanted them left. The driver proceeded to lift them off with the grab attached to the lorry. For some reason Rusty ran over, under the lift of brick and just as he was directly underneath them, the strap holding the brick together snapped, spilling bricks everywhere. Rusty didn't stand a chance. Most of the bale landed on top of him.

"I was numb", said Danny, frozen to the spot. Then I rushed over and started pulling the brick off Rusty. The sight was awful, blood was pouring from several bad wounds, the whole left side of his face was bashed in. One eye was completely gone. He was trying to say something but he just got out one word "Tell" and then nothing more. We cleared the brick from around him, the foreman had already phone for an ambulance but I knew there was nothing could be done.

The lorry driver was going berserk. Sometimes shouting "It wasn't my fault" and neither it was.

Father O'Leary came down and gave him the last rights. I had to go and sit down. I was in total shock, Father O'Leary and the rest of the men done their best to comfort me. Even speaking about it three years later that awful feeling comes flooding back".

As he told Miss Kilfedder the story, tears flooded down his cheek. He stopped and composed himself, then he proceeded to tell Miss Kilfedder about the days and weeks that followed. Hamish insisted Rusty's remains be brought back to Kinlochleven to be buried.

"I started to down the juice at an awful rate to try and forget the whole nightmare", said Danny. "But I'd waken up at night screaming, the sight of Rusty lying there, blood pouring from everywhere, face bashed in and his one eye still staring at me even though he was already dead will never leave me". Father OLeary was very kind to me, he tried his best to get me to slow down on the booze. I couldn't

185

work anymore, the foreman came to see me and tried his best to coax me back but I just couldn't go. I even told him to hold on to our tools, I wouldn't need them anymore".

Danny explained how the days ran into each other, he was exhausted and drained by depression. He thought of going home to Ireland but he realised it wouldn't be a good idea.

"I was company for no one, he said, and certainly not my mother". Time, dragged on, weeks became months. Then he was given notice to vacate his flat.

"I was way behind in rent", said Danny. "As well as that it was still full of Rusty's belongings, clothes and things. My money was well and truly done. I gave the landlord my van to pay off my debt and I told him to get rid of all there was in the flat. As well as Rustys things I had an amount of decent clothes, sports jackets, shirts and shoes. I didn't want any of them. I took one blanket and slept in a park nearby. The weather was fine so I was able to hide the blanket during the day and wrap myself up in it at night. This was ok until there came an awful wet night. So I had to move into a shop door for shelter. Another latchaco was sheltering in the same place. Danny explained to Miss Kilfedder as the rain beat in on top of them the other guy decided he was going to Gin Anne's.

"Who the devil is Gin Annie?" I asked the lad. He explained to me she was a wino but she lived in a cellar of a house belonging to her brother.

"It's not a palace", he said. "But at least we'll have shelter and Annie won't mind, I've got the entrance fee", he joked, tapping a bottle of whiskey.

"Come on, by the way my name is Luke". After travelling through the streets for ten minutes they went down a set of steps. They let themselves in through a door. There was nobody in the house, one desolate bulb half lit up a fairly big room. Danny looked around the place, it was in a horrible shape. There seemed to be only one bed in the corner, a settee, and a couple of chairs around a wobbly table. One door lead to a half functioning toilet and the smell, it would lift the paint, there was another door leading somewhere. After a while a woman with a yellow shopping bag and man landed in. Right away Danny's friend jumped up whiskey bottle half empty in his hand.

"God love you Annie", he said. "We got caught out tonight so if it's alright with you we'll kip here. This is my good pal Duck egg Dooley, you'd want to hear this man singing Johnny Cash numbers".

Danny was about to explain he didn't sing when his mate hit him a kick on his ankle.

Annie stared at him a while, then she spoke, "Are you Irish"?

Before he could speak his new found friend butted in again "County Mayo's best all the way from near Ballina". Annie shook his hand, "Any human being from Mayo is welcome. You can keep your Cork and Kerry blackguards, your Dublin bastards, your Donegal hoors and as for the losers up across the border, shoot the lot of them, give us a bar of I'll walk the line.

Again his friend butted in "Not tonight Annie, sure the poor man has a fierce dose on him but he'll be as right as rain in the morning, here take a slug out of that".

Annie took the whiskey bottle and downed a mouth full, she then handed to the man who had entered with her. Again after slugging a mouthful he passed it to Danny. He swallowed a drop and passed the now near empty bottle to its rightful owner.

Luke finished it off and started singing the song The boys from the county Mayo. "*Far away from the land of the shamrock and heather*

in search of a living in exile we roam

and whenever we have a chance to assemble together

we think of our land where each one had a home

so boys pulled together in all kinds of weather

never show the white feather where ever you go

Act like a brother and help one another

like the stout hearted men from the Co Mayo"

Annie had taken a bottle of spirits out of the yellow bag, she went over to the table and poured a drop into four mugs, not all clean and handed them around. She filled a jug of water and left it on the mantel piece. After a hour or so Annie and the man who hadn't said much went off into the bedroom through a door that Danny previously didn't notice

"Sorry for putting you in a spot about the singing", said Luke. "But if Annie took a spite at you she'd chase you and by heavens there wouldn't be any chance of staying. Anyway Annie won't remember anything about you being a singer in the morning".

"So yourself and Luke seemed to be comfortable in each other's company", commented Miss Kilfedder.

"Aye I must say I was enjoying his company. He was easy to talk to and he seemed to take great interest in me. He queried how I came to be living rough. So I told him I came for a few months about twenty six years ago and I was still here. When I questioned him about how he came to be on the streets he was very vague. He told me he was from Durham but divulged no other information. I had an inkling he was well educated. He said, "I can see your still a novice at this game but tomorrow I'll show you some of the tricks how to survive".

Eventually Luke dozed off. From the half opened bedroom door came muffled passion noises. Danny surveyed his surroundings. How did he sink so low, shacked up in a kip his father wouldn't have put calves in. His depression was worse now than ever, he was at the bottom of a hole, emptiness had sucked all the energy out of him. Would this cursed thing never end? Eventually he dozed off. Sometime later he awakened by a commotion coming from the bedroom, shouting and cursing.

Then the man appeared in a rage, "That's a thieving whore in there", he announced. "Do you know what she done she rose when I was asleep and stole all my money".

As he headed towards the door he shouted back, "May you burn in hell".

Danny didn't stir and Luke seemed to sleep through the whole racket. After a while Luke whispered to Danny, "Say nothing to Annie, pretend you heard nothing".

Five minutes later Annie appeared from the bedroom. "One smart bastard", she said as if speaking to herself. "The last two times he didn't pay me. Gin Annie maybe cheap but not free so now we're even".

Danny then told Miss Kilfedder the next morning he and Luke headed out through the city back streets.

"I'm sure you'd like something to eat", Luke commented. "How long has it been since you've eaten"?

"Twenty four hours", Danny answered. "But it doesn't bother me".

Eventually they entered a building and the smell of food came wafting at them. There was as many as twenty men eating. Several women was serving behind a counter.

"Ach my wee sweetheart Minnie", said Luke to a friendly looking woman. "How's it cutting today"?

"Everyday I see you is a good day", answered Minnie. "You've brought a mate with you.

"Aye this is Duck egg Dooley, all the way from the aul country", said Luke. "Could we have a breakfast each please Minnie".

"Sit down and we'll see what we can do", replied Minnie. When she came down with the food Minnie questioned Danny.

"Where in Ireland are you from?

"The Leitrim Cavan border", Danny answered trying to be as vague as possible.

"I'm from North Donegal myself", said Minnie. "But I know nobody from your place".

After they had eaten and left Luke explained there was quite a few soup kitchens about. "And now we'll get you a few pounds".

They walked a mile or so and then entered a building.

Luke whispered "Let me do the talking". He went up to a girl at a desk. "Good morning Mr Gorman", she said. "What are you after today, surely not more money".

"No, well not for myself", he said. "I'd like you to sort out this poor bloke, he's in bad shape, he had an accident a couple of weeks ago and is unable to work since". Danny decided he'd heard enough so he decided to wait on Luke outside the door.

Ten minutes later Luke stuck his head outside the door, "Come in and sign this form" he said to Danny. "And say nothing". Danny entered and now a second woman was at the desk.

"Mr Gorman says you had an accident", said the second woman. "And you've lost your speech". Danny nodded. After a bit of toing and froing the second woman went to another office and she came back with a form.

"Sign here", she said. Danny gingerly signed it. Back she went into the office and came out with an envelope.

"That's only an emergency if you want anymore assistance we would need more information from you".

As they walked down the street Luke let a great laugh "Do you know Danny you're not a bad conartist. We'll travel to the other side of town and go again".

They took two buses and travelled for about an hour, again they entered an office. After waiting in a crowded waiting room, the same thing happened again, exactly as before.

"That's two twenties", said Luke. "Not brilliant but it'll keep you going for a while".

"We stayed together for a few weeks", Danny told Miss Kilfedder. "He seemed to like me and I must say I found him interesting, I wasn't drinking as much but sometimes when the depression got really bad I'd down a bottle of cheap vodka as I found it made life more bearable".

Luke seemed to drink very little but he knew all the haunts where the rough sleepers and down and outs frequented. It was now three months since Rusty was killed but many nights I still had nightmares of the whole accident.

"It always ended up the same with me frozen to the spot as the bale of brick came crashing down on Rusty and then running over and seeing Rusty's one eye staring back at me I usually ended jumping up screaming".

Danny sat holding his head in his hands.

"So you and Luke spent much time together", asked Miss Kilfedder.

"He seemed to know his way around and knew all the scams that go with that kind of living".

Danny then told Miss Kilfedder how Luke was able to provide fruit, clothes, and even money.

"We'd go in the evening to the markets when the fruit and veg stall holders were packing up, there was always plenty of damaged stock lying about, the stall holders would fill us a bag each, it was handier for them than hauling all back to their store. Charity shops would give us the best of clothes when we'd make sure we'd go in wearing very little. The clothes and fruit and veg we'd bring back to some camp and distribute them. This gave us kudo points and we were well liked, for in some of those places a fierce amount of arguing and fighting took place. As for the money we'd get a tin and sit somewhere busy we'd have a placard with something written on it like "I'm a widower with six children to feed", it's amazing how much we could gather up. We used to have a contest to see who would collect the most. He would sit at one side of the street and I'd be on the other side. Then after a couple of hours we'd meet up and see which of us had the most.

Danny let a giggle. "We also compared notes to see which of us had received the biggest insult".

Danny explained to Miss Kilfedder how Luke would disappear sometimes two or three days at a time Danny reckoned these days were the worst. Then Luke would arrive back in the area, they meet up and his mood would lighten a small bit. Odd nights if the weather was nasty they'd doss down in Gin Annies. There was always something going on there, arguments, fights, singing and even dancing. Danny was well received by Annie and he made sure he'd a bottle of hooch to share. Annie even suggested one night he could share her bed but he gently declined. He'd seen too many rows over the privilege. Then one night a big fella much taller than Danny started to pick at him. This man had taken an notion that Danny was from Scotland. He started to call him offensive names, when Danny didn't respond he started to shove Danny and inviting him to step outside to fight. He kept this up until Danny couldn't take no more. He rose and swung his fist at the same time and caught him on the nose. The man let an outrageous scream and he fell backwards across the table.

Danny rubbed his fist. "That was a big mistake to mess about with me", he yelled.

As he walked out the door he could hear the man whimpering "He's broken my nose" he hung about outside for he knew Luke would follow him.

After twenty minutes Danny and Luke met up. "You're a tough cookie Danny they're trying to stem the blood in there, even though Annie stated she's barred you, that was the right stuff for that guy".

CHAPTER 25

Luke disappeared as usual but this time a few days stretched into a few weeks. Danny searched all the usual haunts to no avail. Again he could find himself sinking into a very deep depression.

"Then one day I was passing a bookshop when I spied the window was full of books with Lukes face on the cover. I went in and lifted a book as if considering buying it. "Down but not out" was the name of it but the authors name was Kenneth Waring, not Luke Gorman. It explained also on the cover how he'd lived six months with the down and outs and rough sleepers in London. I flicked through the pages and came upon photographs, I knew quite a few of the faces including Gin Annie, Beaver and big Sam Noggin. I flicked on through it to the end but I didn't feature".

Danny realised this was the reason why he went missing every so often. He was very disappointed, Luke left and didn't tell him of his true identity. Again he'd lost someone who's company he liked, the weather was fine and he was able to sleep in the park at night. He visited one of the assistance centres and usually received a hand out of twenty pounds. This money he could spend on alcohol. He found out about a few other food banks which he visited once or twice a day and was given a warm meal. One day as he was passing a church he saw people going into it for the service. It struck him it was Sunday and he hadn't phoned his mother for some weeks. He gathered up some change, found a phone box and rang home. Danny hesitated a while before he told Miss Kilfedder what happened next.

"There was no answer which surprised me, where could she be? Bosco usually brought her to Mass but she'd already be home and had her dinner taken. I decided to phone Bosco. I wasn't prepared for what he told me".

"Your Mother he said, your Mother"…….. And when he hesitated I knew it was bad news, "We buried your mother this day fortnight". If I had been hit over the head with a sledge hammer I wouldn't have been more shocked".

Again Danny stopped and took a few breaths before he continued in a low broken voice. "Where the devil are you or why were you not keeping in contact with your mother," said Bosco. "Bosco will you ring me back on this number right away. So he did. Now I was in an awful state. I was sobbing and crying. He told me how he had found her lying on the floor one morning, she had taken a stroke and was lying there all night.

"When we got her to the hospital, the doctors said they couldn't do anything. She died two days later and all the neighbours gather together and we gave her a very respectful burial. We tried hard to get in touch with you, but of course we couldn't". I made an excuse that I was involved in an accident and was in a coma for three weeks".

Danny, Bosco said, "you must come home right away, there is loads of stuff to be sorted out".

Danny now had a dilemma, where was he going to raise the money for the journey, who could he borrow off. If only he could contact Luke, he could maybe help him out. Then it stuck him Father O'Leary, the priest whose church they were working at when Rusty was killed. He walked the few miles to the new church. It was only a few months in use, he knew if he could coax Father O'Leary to give him a loan there'd be a good chance his mother would have left him money so he could pay him back. There was no sign of Father O'Leary but he waited about. An oldish woman came and started to weed a flower bed so he asked her where would he find Fr O'Leary, the woman directed him to the parochial house. He wasn't about but he waited and waited, just as he was about to give up, Father O'Leary arrived. When the padre saw him he threw his arms around him, it was eight months from Rusty was killed and he hadn't come across him since.

Danny explained his dilemma. It took him quite a while for after nearly every sentence he broke down.

"I was in an awful state", said Danny. "Father O'Leary took his time but he said "Danny I'll see you right but I'd need most of it back because I'd have to take it from some other source. As you know we're skint after building the new church". I told him I'd have the whole lot back in a week or so, he gave me four hundred pounds, as I was leaving he give me a big hug.

"I know Danny you a good man and Ill pray you'll be able to get yourself on the straight and narrow".

The trip was long and lonesome. Bosco lifted me in the village. He said that Susan would have the dinner ready and we could have a long chat. He could tell me of my mother's last days".

Bosco told Danny about talking to his mother on the night before he found her on the floor.

"She was in good form", said Bosco. "I'll see you in the morning was the last words she said to me".

He told Danny about finding her and he knew right away she was critical ill so he phoned the doctor and he had an ambulance called before he left home.

"She never really improved," said Bosco. "I sat up with her that night. All night long, she kept repeating where's Dan, tell Danny I want him". One O'clock the next day she went silent and two hours later she was gone".

Bosco explained to Danny how desperately they tried to contact him. His mother had a few numbers under the name of Danny but no one had a clue who they were talking about when they rang them.

"Do you know who was a great help arranging the wake and funeral, Martin and Owenie Carlin remarked Bosco I don't know what we'd have done without them. All went well but of course the one person she'd have wanted to be there wasn't. The priest Father Duggan had great praise for her.

Bosco told Danny how he paid for items which was purchased for the wake but the undertaker and other bills were still outstanding.

"You can stay with us tonight", proposed Bosco. "It's not four star but maybe you weren't used to that standard anyway".

Danny declined "I'll just stay up at home, it won't be easy but I have to stay sometime".

Bosco dropped him off and gave him the key, "I'll talk to you in the morning" he said and moved away.

Danny couldn't bring himself to open the door. This was the first time there was no one there to greet him. Eventually he swallowed deep, opened the door and walked in. The house was as it always was. His Mothers vacant chair was till at one side of the fire. Granny's chair was still on the other side, the wooden chair his father used was still at the top of the table. He didn't like too much heat "Bad for your health" he used to say. As he looked around Danny realised the house and contents was more or less the same as when he left. He had sent money home to install the electric and phone, he also paid to have a bathroom built but apart from that it was the same. He went up to his bedroom and took a look around it. He just couldn't gather up the courage to even peep into his mothers or his granny's bedrooms. He lifted an old diary and flicked through the pages. He read from one of the pages – June 2nd, 1960 *we finished cutting the turf today not sorry weather very hot, me and Bosco are for the pictures with Alice and Susan, should be good. It's a cowboy film "The river of no return" Big match on Sunday.* He smiled for he still remembered both the film and the match against St Pats.

He told Miss Kilfedder "You see I was the star that day but as well my friendship with Alice was nearing an end". He read another page, August 18th *Thinking hard about going back to England with Martin Carlin. Trying to convince Bosco to come but his aul fella has turned nasty. I have two weeks to make up my mind.*

He stared into the ground as he muttered "Jesus if I could only turn back time".

A long silence developed eventually broken by Miss Kilfedder.

"How long did you stay at home Danny?"

"I stayed ten days", answered Danny. "That first night I completely emptied a bottle of rum I had with me, I fell asleep in granny's chair and was wakened by Bosco the next morning at ten o'clock. Susan had sent over a few scones and I made tea. As I had the tea, Bosco announced he was free to bring me wherever I wanted to go".

He told Bosco the first place he wanted to go was to see his mother's grave, then to the solicitors and the undertakers.

He broke down and wept bitterly at the grave side. After a while he read the notes on the wreaths, one was from Bosco and family and the other from the Carlin family. He read the names of his Granny, Granda, and father and the dates they died.

"I wonder could I ask you Bosco to arrange to have my Mother's name added".

"Don't worry it's as good as done", Bosco replied.

Bosco then brought him to the solicitors, "He's anxious to see you", said Bosco.

The solicitor lined out in detail the contents of his Mother's will "As I'm sure you know", he said. "Most of her estate has been left to you. She left the priests of the parish five hundred pounds for masses, she also left money for the missions, Bosco was left a thousand pounds and the rest is yours, I will have it for you in two day's time. It comes to four thousand and seventy pounds".

"I wonder could I have it in cash", Danny asked. "Ive no personal bank account in England only a business one, I'll arrange that", said the solicitor. Danny decided he wouldn't go near the undertaker until he had the money to pay him. Before he struck up with Bosco again he purchased two bottles of whiskey.

"I'm sure these days were very stressful for you", said Mrs Kilfedder.

"Awful altogether" answered Danny "I was running on empty, I could happily lay down in the corner and died. When I woke up in the morning I just didn't know how I was going to get through the day. The only good thing was Bosco seemed to understand and gave me good support without suffocating me".

For the next few days Danny didn't do much, just sat in the house with his thoughts. Every now and then he'd take a stroll around the fields but usually a memory of something which happened in these places would come flooding back. He would just turn back and go into the house and have another glass of whiskey.

Miss Kilfedder queried him on some of the memories that made him turn back to the house again.

"For instance I came across the large flat stone in the back field", said Danny, and remembered sitting on it one evening deciding should I go to England. I had a clear picture in my head what I wanted to do. I'd come over here for a few years, earn enough money to make life handier for myself and parents back on the farm. It was a brilliant idea if I'd stuck to it, but ……. Another evening I wandered into another field. Again I remember clearly cutting corn, this was a year before I had taken the notion of coming here. It was a fine harvest day, it was always my favourite time of the year, harvest time. I was going dancing that night. I had an important football match on Sunday and I remember thinking I couldn't be happier. I hadn't a worry in the world".

Miss Kilfedder could hear Danny's voice breaking. He fell silent for a while but then continued to tell her of the next few days. Bosco always brought him over a breakfast in the morning and stayed for a chat. Bosco never probed Danny too much about his life in England this last number of years. Then one morning he casually asked Danny about what his plans were, was he thinking of staying at home?

"I just blurted all out", Danny told Miss Kilfedder. "I told Bosco I wasn't in a good place, I wasn't sure what life held for me. I told him I didn't think I could stay at home and I wasn't sure if England was the best place for me.

Bosco said he realised I wasn't at my best and wondered if I should seek help. I told him I some how would get over it myself. Then I told him I owed a man over in London money and I'd have to pay him back".

Danny then told Bosco in detail about Anouskia. How they met, how much they loved each other and how cruelly she was taken from him.

"I was bringing her home to meet you all. Now that was going to be the proudest moment of my life, introducing her to my mother and father and the rest of you. We'd decided we wouldn't tell anyone, a complete surprise. I know for sure mummy and daddy would have loved her". "Oh! my God" exclaimed Bosco "why did you not mention this girl before. She seemed to be the love of your life".

"I couldn't mention her explained Danny because it was too raw and do you know Bosco it's still too raw, seven years later; that is the basis of my problem".

"Bosco could see I was getting upset", Danny told Miss Kilfedder. So he suggested I come with him on a journey to lift a part for his tractor. "Then we can call with the solicitors and collect your money and visit your mother's grave".

"And that's what we did and I called and paid the undertaker, of course I had a bottle of spirits home with me".

Miss Kilfedder decided to probe a little more on his friendship with Anouskia "Did you and Anouskia live together?" she asked Danny. "No, not all the time", he replied. "She had her own flat above the bar where she worked. I was working quite a bit out of London. Then we'd meet up on Friday night and spend the weekend together. Oh! the joy of being together after 5 days apart was the best feeling in the world. We'd make love for hours until we were exhausted. On Saturdays we'd wander around the shops maybe take in a show or go for a meal. In the summer we'd drive away out into the country, book into a quiet hotel and spend the time wandering around little back roads hand in hand giggling like teenagers. The world was a much brighter place when we were together, problems shrank and no matter how intorable work was during the week, a smile, hug and kiss, from Anouskia banished all worries.

"Had you made any plans to marry?" Miss kilfedder asked.

"Ach no, we were afraid it might change things, our lives were so wonderful, just perfect".

Danny was silent again. Then he gave a sigh, "Perfect one minute, all over the next".

"It must have been horrendous", Miss Kilfedder commented.

"It's something I'll never get over no matter how long I live", Danny replied.

"Anouskia's body was taken back to Sweden but I just hadn't the energy to travel out there. I didn't even go to the morgue. I still had this notion, she'd come bouncing through the door at any moment. Two of her brothers came over to bring her body back home. They tried to coax me to go over with them but no I couldn't. They said the whole family would like to meet me, because Anouskia told them many times about this wonderful Irish man she'd fell in love with".

After taking a few more notes Miss Kilfedder asked Danny did he have any company in the days that followed.

"Apart from the two lads who had worked with me, there was no one else. I was only a short time, maybe eight months in that particular part of the city, and spending any spare time with Anouskia left me not having to make friends. The two lads finished the job we were working on. I told them I wasn't near ready to resume work. I had another job to start so I told them to meet the contractor and explain to him they would be doing the job.

So that's what happened.

"You never thought of going home to Ireland", Miss Kilfedder enquiried "Yes at the start I did" I would loved to have my mother's arms around me, comforting me, telling me everything will work out but the more I studied it I came to the conclusion it wasn't a good idea. You see I hadn't told my parents much about Anouskia, just snippets. Maybe after I'd come on the phone I'd say she was a girl I took out the odd time. I was waiting to surprise them. About four days after Anouskia was killed I rang my mother it was my usual time on a Sunday. I kept calm as I could, even though I wanted to blurt out all that had happened, tell them I'd lost my soulmate but I knew I would annoy them immensely so I just passed the remark, I had known a girl who had been killed in a car bomb, that was it. When I came off the phone I screamed as loud as I could to rid myself of the tension that had built up inside me".

Danny explained to Miss Kilfedder how he spent the weeks and months ahead.

"I sat in a trance, stunned and apart from going to the chippie and corner shop for food I never moved out. Lucky enough I had plenty of money saved up. After about four weeks I started going down to the pub about once a week, I'd have maybe two pints. I seldom had a conversation with anyone. Some nights I might see a young couple in there laughing and joking just like Anouskia and myself used to do. I might be on my first pint and I'd leave what was left and go home".

"So you weren't drinking very heavily", Miss Kilfedder queried.

"Not at first", said Danny, "but one night when I left early, I brought a bottle home a bottle of brandy. I consumed a few glasses of it and found it lightened my mood so I started drinking more regularly".

Danny then related to Miss Kilfedder, how he found his mood changing a little bit

. "I started going for walks during the day, it was now May and the weather was fine. My first place to call was the local church. I'd go in and say a prayer to Anouskia asking her to help me. I always kept with me a pair of Rosary beads my

Granny gave me the day I left home, somehow it's done me a world of good".

Danny went on to explain how on one of his walks he stopped to chat to a woman who was working at a flower bed in her garden. As he was leaving she asked him if he knew anyone who would erect a fence at the bottom of her garden.

"Before I knew it, I'd agreed I would do the work, I still had my van and any amount of tools so I started the very next day. Maude the house owner was delighted. She carried a considerable amount of refreshments. During one of these stoppages she enquired more into my background so I told her everything that had happened to me she was genuinely sympathetic".

"How did it feel to have resumed work?" Miss Kilfedder asked.

"I must say it was a great help, instead of sitting feeling sorry for myself I was planning the best way to tackle this job".

After Danny had the fence completed Maude got him to dig up part of the garden and construct a flower bed. Maude was a nice friendly lady and Danny could see strands of his mother in her. One day Maude's work was coming to an end, another woman arrived to see if Danny could lay a path for her. Again this lady treated Danny well. Now others were enquiring from Maude about her handy man as they had small jobs to do.

"So on it went, all summer", said Danny. "I was fairly reliable and I done the work at a reasonable cost. I must say I enjoyed those summer months. Every morning I always called into the church and had a little chat with Anouskia, for as far as I was concerned it was her who had made my life bearable again.

Miss Kilfedder looked at her watch. "I'm afraid Danny we've come to the end of this session but I'll see you again tomorrow at the same time. Any questions?"

"No but I want to thank you for listening to me, I must say I find it comforting telling my story to you".

"That's my job Danny" said Miss Kilfedder. "And I'm delighted you find it helpful, you're still taking your medication I hope".

Danny hesitated before answering "I am but to be honest with you I don't think it's doing me any good".

"But Danny you are only here two weeks", Miss Kilfedder replied. "It's a miracle your looking for, your course is at the minimum six weeks and if you're not showing a vast improvement by then we can extend it".

"We", said Danny sarcastically.

"Look Danny, where you believe it or not we are experts in this field. Every year we treat dozens of Danny's, Ive seen so many come in here in a worse state than you reluctant to cooperate and walk out six or eight weeks later different person. It's really up to you Danny. The old saying applies "No pain no gain". Mr Rodgers is the top psychiatrist in the business and if you want to be cured he'll give it one mighty try".

As she goes towards the door she gives Danny a pat on the shoulder "See you tomorrow at two".

CHAPTER 26

"Yesterday we ended your discussion by you saying how much you enjoyed doing the small jobs for people", said Miss Kilfedder.

"Yes", replied Danny. "I thoroughly enjoyed it, it made me think, think how I'd approach some of these jobs. Work out how to go about doing them. The big drawback was the weekends. No matter how hard I tried not to think about the past it seemed to hit me on Friday evening, this was the part of the weekend I spent with Anouskia, on my way home on Friday I could find my mood getting darker. I always ended up buying alcohol. All weekend I'd spend in a drunken stupor. Sometimes I was in such poor shape I'd miss going to work on Monday".

"Did you confine your drinking to the weekend?" asked Miss Kilfedder. "Yes since I was back at work, talking to the people I was doing jobs for, I was usually was fine".

"So this continued all summer", remarked Miss Kilfedder. "What prompted you to quit?"

"As the summer and autumn faded, around the middle of October, the jobs dried up. Nobody wanted me then I found myself back sitting in the flat. The longer I sat the harder I found it to go out, even for a walk".

"You never thought of going home", Miss Kilfedder queried.

"I couldn't", answered Danny. "They would have guessed I wasn't my usual self I always phoned as usual on Sundays at seven o'clock, tried to sound cheery and normal I told them I was so busy all summer I left going home to Christmas. My father had cut back on farming and they'd lapsed into a nice quiet style of life".

Danny explained to Miss Kilfedder how his mood would lighten enough some days so he could go for a walk.

"I would find a park and casually ramble around it. Other days I'd drive to somewhere on the banks of the Thames and watch the boats and rafts sailing up and down".

Miss Kilfedder left down her pen "You didn't at any time have any silly thoughts regarding the river", Danny seemed surprised. "What do you mean, commit suicide. No matter how dark things were that never crossed my mind. How could I, imagine the affect that would have on mummy and daddy".

"Was it around this time you teamed up with Rusty"? Enquired Miss Kilfedder. "One day I was passing a building site, a new hotel, this large fella with ginger hair was down near the entrance laying paving brick. I stood watching him work. After a while he straightened up and came up to me. We talked a few minutes and I told him I was paver myself. After finding out I wasn't working he told me he was desperately looking for a mate. Would I be interested? I said I'd consider it and tell him the next day, the rest as they say is history. From day one as I told you before we just clicked, enjoyed each other's company. He was big, brash and loud but behind it all there was a gentle side to him".

"Did you go home at Christmas?", enquired Miss Kilfedder.

"Yes I went over but before I went I gave Rusty instructions to phone me on Boxing Day and say I was urgently required back to sign a contract so that I didn't have to stay too long. All went as planned, I spent Christmas with my parents and was back after four days".

Danny told Miss Kilfedder how he and Rusty seemed to gel from the start. He could feel his mood changing. After a month or so they moved in together. They worked hard and after every job, partied hard, often for a week or so. Rusty was usually placid but now and again a vicious streak in him showed up.

"We found ourselves in many rows", said Danny. "And the bigger the opposition the more he liked it. Many times we were barred from pubs and told never to come back".

"How long were you together"? asked Miss Kilfedder. "Four years", answered Danny. "We had some good times both at work and play. Everywhere we went, building sites or bars, Rusty was the life of the place. Sometimes when I'd felt he went too far, maybe caused a row, I'd say to him I'd be better off without him. He'd say "Ach! Danny we're a great team, we would be no good without each other". "And so it was proved when he was killed".

Miss Kilfedder decided to find out what took place the last visit to Ireland after his mother had died.

"I received the money my mother had left me from the solicitors, a little over four thousand pounds. I gave Bosco a thousand to pay for items he bought to put over the wake and give some to anyone who helped at the wake".

Danny related to Miss Kilfedder, how he'd taken his mother's bicycle and cycled different places.

"The first place I went was down to Pat Burkes, standing looking down the lane, I could remember well the mixed up feelings I had watching Emma heading down the lane in the taxi. Emma returned only once after that. She was on her honeymoon. Another shattered dream of mine".

He walked around the yard, opening every door and peering inside. Little had changed from when he'd looked after Pats stock before the auction. He remembered the awful row he had with the Rook Ruddy over the spade Emma gave to Johney Brennan. He searched the hay shed where Johney had hidden it behind some hay. Both the hay and spade were gone. He wandered up the back lane and the fields beyond. Nostalgic filled his brain, looking back it was all so innocent between Emma and himself, but he was disappointed, Emma didn't indicate she hadn't taken the whole affair serious. He travelled on to the back field and looked down on the far corner where he and Emma had watched the rabbits. Almost as if instructed, just for old times sake, a couple of rabbits appeared and skipped about.

"There, Danny thought life around the world reaches different conclusions but the wild life on Pat Burkes farm stays the same".

Another day as he cycled past Edmund Coyle's place. A man was standing at the entrance to a large dwelling. There was nothing left of Edmunds farmyard. His mother had told Danny, the place was sold soon after Edmund passed away and sold on several times since.

"It's an English couple, his mother told him, who owns it now as far as I know. They don't mix". The man at the gate didn't acknowledge Danny in any way. He smiled to himself at the idea of Edmunds farm being owned by an English man.

"You see", Danny explained to Miss Kilfedder, "Edmund hadn't a great liking for anyone on this side of the Irish sea. "Heathens every one of them he'd say".

He travelled on around the road to where Johney the Spade dwelled (Danny explained to Miss Kilfedder who these individuals were as they appeared in his story and how they fitted into his life before he left home). In the early years he would meet and always have a laugh with Johney. It would have been ten years since he saw him. The door of Johneys house was open so he entered. In a darkened corner near the fire sat Johney, now well into his eighties. Dark and all as the house was Johney recognised him.

"Ach! Danny, how are you getting on?"

"Grand", answered Danny. "And how are you?"

"Killed with pains Danny, too much hard work on long summer days and cold wet winters. I'm afraid I didn't make it to your mothers wake or funeral". "No harm Johney sure I didn't make to it myself", said Danny.

They talked about old times Danny told Johney about looking for the spade. "That was some handling over that", said Johney. "And I never went back for it". Danny reminded Johney about the time he purchased the new watch. Johney laughed hearty and kept slapping his knee.

"Your mother and father missed you Danny when you left", he said. "And to tell you the truth Danny I missed you too. We used to have good fun".

When Danny made to leave Johney shuffled to the door "I suppose you'll hardly stay about".

"I'll probably head back in a day or so", answered Danny. "Well good luck to you Danny", said Johney. "I'll probably not see you again".

"Who knows", said Danny. "Who knows".

He cycled round past Cassie Byrnes house, now derelict. Cassie kept the catalogue going for a few years but a few clients didn't complete their payments and left Cassie in debt. Danny remembered his mother telling him of her passing a long time ago.

"She was still a young woman about sixty", said his mother "But those blackguards who didn't stick to their commitments affected her health".

Danny with his head bowed was silent. Miss Kilfedder decided to extract more of his story from him.

"How long did you stay at home"? she asked.

"Every night I came back from having my dinner in Bosco's I felt terrible an aloneness" said Danny. "Everything had changed completely. Most of the older people were dead and folk of my own age were married and had different commitments. Even Bosco now with a wife and three children to cater for, had a completely different lifestyle".

Danny envied Bosco and one day he told Bosco how lucky he was to have a family.

Bosco giggled, "I suppose I am, though at times when they come between me and Susan I could see them far enough, there's a constant want in them".

"Maybe so, said Danny, but never forget Bosco they're the future, you'll watch and be as proud as they get educated and settle into jobs. You'll walk your two daughters no doubt up the isle when they marry. As the grandchildren come along you'll take great delight in seeing them grow, the future continuing. Then take me". Bosco tried his best to raise Danny's spirits. "Your still a young man, there's no reason you won't have this someday".

"That night at home I decided I'd go back in a few days". The next day I took the bus down to the solicitors, I told him I wanted to make my will. It was simple enough I told him I wanted to leave the farm to Bosco if anything should happen to me".

A few days later Bosco left him to the bus. It was a Sunday and they came upon Martin and Owenie Carlin on the road. There were three children with them. Danny bade Bosco to stop.

They exchanged greetings. "I would like to thank you for helping at my Mothers wake", said Danny. "Bosco said you were mighty".

"Ach! sure it was the least we could do", said Martin. "Your mother was a great woman".

After they pulled away Danny enquired which of them owned the children Bosco told him Martin had two and Owenie had three.

"The two older lads would be away playing football". Danny asked Bosco what were Martin and Owenies circumstances, Bosco told him, both had done well for themselves. Martin had took over the running of the insurance brokers he worked for and now it was the largest about. Owenie married a girl whose father ran an equipment hire business and seemed to be one of the main men. Both had built fine houses for themselves. Before they departed at the bus station Bosco assured Danny he was welcome at his house anytime. "I have the rent money for the land to pay you in a few months' time".

"I'll call for it sometime just hold on to it until then", said Danny. "I have enough for now". Danny sat silently head bowed. "Now that you were back again", queried Miss Kilfedder. "How did that feel"?

Danny rubbed his head "I went straight away and paid Father O'Leary back his money and I gave him another £500 to keep for me. I told him I'd probably come looking for it in a short while". It'll always be there for you Danny", said Fr O'Leary. "But please try and work out some pattern to your life Danny". Danny agreed with Fr O'Leary he'd need to do something. When he had all paid he still had £1230. He hoped this would see him through until he'd find a job, although work wasn't near as plentiful as years back. He found a small cellar bedsit. It was a dimly light and just had the bare necessaries a bed, a gas cooker and a shared bathroom.

"The night I moved in I sat in the semi dark watching people's feet, the only part of them I could see pass the window and suddenly it stuck me, my mother the last while in her life wouldn't have been any better off. Sitting in her chair wondering what was going to happen to her. I fell into the bed tears streaming down my face. I had a full bottle of whiskey and I drained it in less than an hour. I conked out and it was midday before I wakened, feeling wretched".

Danny tried his best to make his situation better but found it very hard. Weeks past without any improvement. Now he was drinking more eating next to nothing. When he became half sober his depressive state took over so back he went to alcohol.

"I tried to find a job but anyone looking at me knew I couldn't hold down a job. I did get a start with a contractor. The first day the foreman sent me to clean out the gutter of a house. I gingerly climbed a set of steps but as I reached up to the gutter my head started to spin, before I knew it I was lying on the ground. The foreman, in his early twenties came rushing around the corner roaring as he went. "Take yourself out of here you drunk, before you kill yourself or worse still someone else". Can you imagine, some young whippet who I wouldn't have seen in my way a few years back, telling me to clear off, but I knew myself I couldn't stay and work a full day".

It wasn't long before Danny found himself running out of money. He called with Father O'Leary and received two hundred pounds of the money he left with him. Father O'Leary talked to him and advised him to try and turn his life around. "Danny, you never thought of looking for treatment. I know a specialist very well and I could have a word with him, if you would agree, and find out if he'll see you".

Danny rubbed his chin "Ach Father I'm going to make a big effort, I still think I can turn things around on my own".

"And did you make any progress"? asked Miss Kilfedder.

"Well I suppose not much", Danny replied. "I did find a job with a landscape gardener. The first day was as long as a week. I couldn't wait until quitting time, but about an hour before we were due to finish the boss announced we'd have to stay on a few hours to finish the job. I threw the rake I was using as far as possible, left and never went back. I went to my dingy room below the ground with a cheap bottle of booze and stayed in bed for three days".

Danny soon visited Father O'Leary again and received the last of his money.

"Look", said Father O'Leary. "I like you a lot Danny, I know you come from fine stock and it breaks my heart to see you this way, please try and sort yourself out, and that offer of me talking to a specialist still stands. If you feel you need help just call me and I'll try to arrange a meeting with this man".

Danny agreed he would.

After a long pause Miss Kilfedder spoke "What led up to you eventually going back to Father O'Leary?"

"My depression was now worse than ever" I lay in bed day after day, I just didn't have the energy to get up. I wasn't eating and when I did make a terrible effort, I made it to the shops and stocked up on booze and some, but not much food. I was often in a trance for days, sometimes my brain would clear a tiny bit but, wicked thoughts would flood back again. Sometimes they'd be of Anouskia or Rusty covered in brick pavers and his one eye still staring at me, then there was my mother. Poor mammy sitting in the corner all alone. Nobody of her own to give her a smile or a warm word. Wondering what was going to be the end of her. She stood up so often in my youth, no matter what I did. She'd never scold me, always took my side. Then in her hour of need I wasn't there to hold her weary hand".

Miss Kilfedder could hear Danny sobbing as he held his head in his hands. After a minutes silence Miss Kilfedder ventured "You decided to take Father O'Leary up on his offer".

"Not right away ", Danny replied. "My money lasted about four weeks; then one night the landlord came looking for three month's rent which I didn't have. I cleared out my pockets in front of him, I had the princely sum of fourteen pounds. He gathered it up and before he left he warned me to either have the rest for the next morning or be gone. So there was nothing for it but to go back to the streets again. Lucky enough it was the summer and the weather was good".

Danny tried the assistance office but the girl explained the regulations had changed and he wouldn't be eligible for help. He was given food at a food station but with no money to purchase booze he became increasingly desperate. He visited some of the old haunts he'd frequented before, but when the occupants realised he had no bottle of his own they became suspicious he might steal someone else's. Then one night, he couldn't stick it any longer, he decided come morning he'd visit Father O'Leary, and take him up on his offer.

"After a phone call or two I landed here" "I can assure you Danny you made the right decision", said Miss Kilfedder. "If you are willing to co-operate we'll do our best to help you" (she looked at her watch) "I'm afraid Danny that's all for today. As I told you a few days ago I'm on my annual leave from this afternoon I'll not see you until tomorrow two weeks". "Lucky you", muttered Danny. "Maybe I could go with you".

Miss Kilfedder let a giggle knowing Danny was only joking "I don't think that would be possible, I'm going with my two sisters to camp in France and they might have something to say if I turned up with a man. Anyway you must stay here and continue your treatment. I'll be talking to Mister Rogers later on; he or some of the other councillors will call with you every day and keep a check on your progress. Keep taking your medication and I'll be looking forward to seeing you in a few weeks.

She goes to shake Danny's hand. "Thanks again Miss Kilfedder, I reckon talking to you makes me feel better than all the other medication put together", said Danny. "Well then we'll continue talking when I return" Miss Kilfedder replied.

"Enjoy your break, you need it, listening to creatures like me, remarked Danny.

CHAPTER 27

After a disturbing night's sleep, Danny lay in bed the next morning contemplating his future. He felt wretched. If only he had some alcohol it might dull the pain. It bothered him also that he wouldn't be seeing Miss Kilfedder for two weeks. He found her a great help, so gentle and understanding genuinely interested and sympathetic towards his story. Her Christian name was Roberta but Mr Rodgers introduced her as Miss Kilfedder and since then that's how he addressed her. She seemed to Danny to be around thirty two or three years old.

Again, not for the first time Danny tried to envisage what the future for him would consist of. What would happen to him when this treatment had ended? Could he live in a hostel, find a job and more or less start over again? Would he find himself back on the streets again?

"That would not be an option", he thought. His mind turned to home. Maybe that's where his future lay. From the last time he was back, he knew a lot had changed from away back when he left, thirty two years ago. Bosco and all his mates were married, rearing families. To the young ones he would be eccentric old man, someone to pick fun at. Anyway, he still had at least three weeks treatment and unless it improves his spirits dramatically it wouldn't matter where he went or stayed.

Father O'Leary was just finished his breakfast one morning about ten days later when the doorbell rang, when he opened the door he was surprised to see Danny there "Ach! Hello Danny" said Fr O'Leary. "I didn't expect to see you here, how's the form"? "Feeling much better", answered Danny. "I just called round to tell you I'm heading back to Ireland today".

Father O'Leary looked puzzled "Oh! I thought your treatment wouldn't be completed for a few weeks yet". "Well, I'd have another week or so to do but I've improved so well these last few weeks I suggested I'd like to go home to Ireland. They told me they'd give me the rest of my medication home with me as long as I promised to take it", Danny replied.

"I must say you looking much brighter" commented Father O'Leary. "And I said before, I thought Ireland might be the best place for you. When are you travelling"?

"I'm taking the train to the boat in a few hour's time and sail over tonight. My friend Bosco will lift me at the far side", Danny replied.

"What about money"? asked Father O'Leary. "Remember I said I wouldn't see you wanting". Danny let a laugh. "I suspected you'd think I was looking for a loan, but no, Bosco sent me over as much as will see me across, thank you all the same Father. I want to thank you for the great help you've been and when Ive settled down I'll send you over a few pounds, I'm sure you have still money owing on the new church".

"I'll not refuse any help I get", said Father O'Leary. "That is another reason for calling with you, I need your address and phone number in case I'd want to contact you".

"Surely, come in and I'll write it down for you." I'll be staying with Bosco for a few weeks; I'll have a few repairs to do to the old homestead so I'll give you Bosco's phone number in case you'd want to contact me". "Well, that's fine. I suppose there's no harm of me having it" noted Father O'Leary. "I'll thank you again for what you have done for me I will always appreciate it", said Danny. Father O'Leary shook Danny's hand. "It was nothing really, I'm so glad to see you're on the mend. Your mood has definitely brightened a lot. I hope you find contentment back in Ireland and who knows you may come back and see us all someday".

"You'd never know", replied Danny.

"It's a grand time of year to be in Ireland, harvest time", said Father O'Leary. "I was reared on a farm in Carlow and I thought the harvest time was a great time of year. The lovely golden colour of the cornfields, there's a particular scent of them. The farmers are all in a fine mood after caring all year for their crops now it was time to gather them in and hap them up for winter. Do you know Danny, I envy you going back home. Best of luck Danny whatever you do I'll say a prayer or two for you".

Three days later was a Sunday. Father O'Leary carried out his routine he had followed for years. After saying Mass he bought the Sunday papers on the way home. After breakfast he always read the papers. On the inside page, he noticed a headline and as he began to read the article he gasped with shock.

"Police said a post-mortem on the body recovered from the Thames will be carried out. The remains are understood to be that of an Irishman, Daniel Higgins who was seen on

Thursday afternoon jumping from the Tower Bridge. It is understood he was in his early fifties. A police spokesperson last night said "enquiries are continuing and a post-mortem examination will be carried out in due course to determine the cause of death".

Father O'Leary was completely stunned "There must be some mistake", he kept repeating to himself. "There has to be". He left here a couple of hours earlier in fine shape. "Was there something in his manner I missed", he thought. "Something I should have seen". He had just started to read the article again when the phone rang, it was his friend, psychiatrist, George Rodgers.

"Did you hear Father about Danny"? he asked.

"Ive just read about it in the paper minutes ago", answered Father O'Leary. "There has to be some mistake, for he called with me on Thursday morning, to tell me he was leaving, going back to Ireland. I never remember him in such a good mood I remember thinking Blue Skies had made a brilliant job of him. What happened, maybe it was an accident".

"I'm afraid not", said George. "We find this happens quite a lot. Anyone intent on suicide will plan everything in minute detail and I mean everything. Danny probably would have decided the exact spot where he'd jump. He probably had some reason for calling with you. Nobody in Blue Skies saw him leave that morning. We thought he might still be in the grounds, maybe fallen asleep somewhere". "Now that you mention that, he asked me for my address and phone number", said Father O'Leary. And something that I felt odd at the time, he insisted on giving me his Irish friend, Bosco's phone number. I suppose he knew I would phone and tell Bosco the tragic news". "Yes and why he asked for your address and phone number was not to raise any suspicion by giving you Bosco's number", replied George. "As well, when they've made the final arrangements their mood lightens. They knew they won't have to wake up another day to do battle with the dark savage beast that's inside their brain".

"I'm devastated", said Father O'Leary. "Maybe there were signs I should have seen on Thursday morning". No! no! a person in that state of mind can fool us all", answered George. "The one I feel sorry for is Roberta Kilfedder she's away on holiday and won't be back to late this evening. She's back at work in the morning. She had taken a particular interest in Danny. Before she left on holiday she told me she thought Danny was beginning to respond to treatment. She'll be so disappointed".

"What a loss". Father O'Leary replied. Why did he have to go down that road, I'm still in deep shock. What happen's now George"?

"Well as it was reported in the paper there will be a post-mortem", answered Mr Rodgers. "At least with him giving you his friend's phone number in Ireland we have someone to contact as I'm sure that was his intention. There's a good chance he'll want to bring his remains back home. Not that he had many but the few items he had we'll gather up and send them back as well. Oh! by the way we come across an open envelope in his locker with your name on it Father. Inside was a set of rosary beads and a note saying, Take good care of these beads Father, they were very precious to me. I'll bring them around to you in due course".

"Ah now! Said Father O'Leary, "he told me about those beads, his grandmother give them to him the day he left Ireland and he explained to me no matter where he went those beads were always in his pockets and when the going got tough he found great comfort gently touching them with his fingers".

After assuring Father O'Leary he'd be back in touch with him in the coming days, Mr Rodgers rang off. Father O'Leary with tears in his eyes, lit a candle, knelt down and prayed.

In the peaceful hollow of Pat Burkes back field the sun shone, three rabbits appeared, skipped around and played.

THE END

Printed and bound by CPI Group (UK) Ltd, Croydon, CR0 4YY